A BRIDE FOR THE RANCH HAND

WESTERN DESTINIES

BLYTHE CARVER

1

———

Sophia Carter looked up as her miniature charge—a short, plump two-and-a-half-year-old baby boy named Felix—came stumbling toward her. He had learned to walk a long time ago but often got ahead of himself and went a little too fast, resulting in a comical display as he hurried to get his balance.

"Whoa, whoa, whoa there," she said with a laugh, putting out one hand. It wouldn't have hurt if he had fallen at that moment. He might have fallen on her, but that would have been fine. If he'd hit the floor, he still would have been cushioned by the thick rug his father had put in the nursery just for this very purpose. The first bruise on his firstborn, Peter's, head and the rug had appeared the next day.

Sophia worked as a nanny and caretaker for Peter, who was affectionately referred to as Muddy, and Felix, and their eleven-month-old brother Collin. They were the children of her employers, Dylan and Mattie Sullivan. Dylan was the silent partner of Luke Turner, who ran the magazine that had brought Sophia to Bighorn, Texas, in the first place.

Sophia's journey to Bighorn had been tumultuous enough that anyone else might have fled the growing city in late 1875. But Sophia was resilient, independent, and a free-thinking woman. She believed that her troubles had made her a stronger woman. She had done what she thought was right to her own detriment on a few occasions, but all had worked out in the end.

She had found steady employment with a delightful couple and was still in contact with the woman she previously worked for, Lydia Green Brinkman. Now the sheriff's wife for several years, Lydia was still her good friend. Bighorn was a large city of ten thousand people, but Lydia still managed to find time to seek out Sophia and take her for ice cream on a hot summer's day.

Felix fell into Sophia, who laughed in delight

and tickled the boy. He spun around, laughing. He was quickly more aggressive than Sophia could handle, and she gave him a good grip, a signal to calm down.

Felix instantly relaxed and *played dead* on her lap.

"Oh, dear," Sophia said in a serious tone, staring down at Felix's limp body in case he was watching through slitted lids. "I do believe I have killed him. His father will not be a happy man." She poked him lightly in his exposed tummy. He reacted slightly, but they both pretended he hadn't.

"Hello?" she asked, poking him again, this time in one shoulder. He managed to keep his face blank. She hesitated to build suspense and then began poking him all over. "Wake up, wake up, wake up, wake up..." she repeated the phrase with each poke, laughing when he screamed, twisted, and scrambled away from her. His laughter rang through the room, drawing the attention of the baby, who was lying on the rug near Sophia, staring at a soft shapeless star his mother had sewn together for him. It was a bright color of yellow, but the baby had been chewing on it, and his new teeth had pulled out a stitch. The insides were slowly coming out. Sophia had taken the star from him several times, but Muddy kept giving it back to him.

With one hand on Felix, pretending to grab at his legs as he made his way away from her, she took the ripped star from the baby with the other.

"How did you get that again?" she asked in a curious voice. "Every time I turn around, you have this. I understand you want me to fix it, but I wish you would find another way of reminding me. You're going to choke on these little pieces, now, aren't you?" She held up some of the insides that had come out of the little star pillow.

"All right, all right," she murmured. "I'll sew it together for you."

"Sophia," Felix cried out her name as if she said she was leaving forever. "Sophia."

Sophia loved the way he dropped the "f" sound in her name and used a "p" instead. It was adorable.

"I'm not leaving you, Felix," Sophia said with a laugh, pushing against the child, who was now clinging to her leg. "All right, just come with me, then."

She walked with the little boy clinging to one leg, swinging him dramatically, which made him cry out with delight. She went to the cupboard by the large window and pulled open the door. The shelves were lined with different repair tools, a small sewing kit being one of them. She took the kit off the shelf and closed the door.

As soon as it swung shut, her eyes went out the window beyond it to the front courtyard in front of the large mansion. Mattie and Dylan Sullivan lived in one wing of the tremendously large house owned by Mattie's father, the judge. The buggy carrying Mattie, Dylan, and their four-year-old, was returning from the doctor's visit.

They might soon know if there was anything wrong with Muddy, who had been feeling strange recently. His parents, and Sophia, and the other nanny who cared for the children, a capable and sweet young woman named Lucy Caldwell, had not been able to ascertain what it was exactly that had the child behaving the way he was.

Sophia and Mattie had discussed his behavior several times. They had agreed that it was probably something Dr. Farnsworth wouldn't be able to diagnose. It wasn't an illness in his body. It was in his mind. It was affecting his judgment, perception, and learning.

He was exceptionally smart for his age, a character even at "nearly five," as he'd been saying since a week after he'd turned four.

Sophia was glad to see them returning. Her heart sped up just a little, anxious to know what Dr. Farnsworth had recommended.

2

Owen Bell stepped out of the mansion and looked out at the horizon. It was clear. No sign that there was any weather coming.

Despite the visual reassurance, Owen knew the almanac wasn't wrong. It had been right about every other major storm that had hit Bighorn for the last five years. He'd recorded it himself, keeping track of his almanacs and never throwing them away so he could track the patterns and do his own calculations where the weather was concerned.

It was important to him in his line of business. He had to make sure all the animals in his care were taken in if a storm was coming. He warned the people he worked for and battened down the hatches.

Owen had spent the last twenty-nine years of his life working for wealthy ranch owners, making sure the property was safe and well maintained. He got rid of poachers with the same enthusiasm as he milked the cows if he happened to be on a farm.

He'd spent the last six months working for Judge Carter Holbrook at his mansion. Most of his work had been on the outside, but every now and then, he went inside to do repairs on broken doors or stairs or after a bizarre accident that left something broken.

He'd seen a very pretty maid that first day, dark hair, bright eyes the color of teal, like the sea, sharp as could be. He could tell she had a brain in that head of hers. He never said anything to her. He just admired her from afar.

It wasn't because Owen wasn't confident in himself. He was, in fact, one of the most confident people he knew. And he made sure to keep his ego in check so that others around him didn't take him for an arrogant man. There was a difference, and he strove to make people understand that.

He shaded his eyes when turning his head, as the afternoon sun was dipping slightly into the west, indicating it was about two in the afternoon. Owen looked up and around, back and forth, and thought to himself, *It's two seventeen.*

Quickly, he whipped out his watch and tapped the button to expose the face. The second hand had just tipped over the sixty-second mark, making it exactly two-seventeen in the afternoon.

Pride filled Owen, and he grinned mischievously.

"What are you doing?"

The sound of his boss's confused voice rang through his ears, and he slid his pocket watch away with a slip of his fingers.

"Sorry, boss," he said hurriedly. "Was just checking the time."

The friendly smile on Dylan's face put Owen back at ease. His shoulders relaxed. He wasn't normally tense around Dylan or the judge, but he didn't like to give the impression he was standing around wasting time. To Owen, time was the most precious thing there was. Next to air. If either of those ran out, life was over.

He pointed toward the horizon.

"I know you want to have this party outside, boss," he remarked, jumping right into business, "but I'm telling you a storm is coming from down that way, and we've got to take precautions."

Dylan had heard this before. When he'd brought up the party to the staff and given a date for when it would be held, Owen had checked his almanac, as usual, to see what the weather would be like that day. He was in charge of the outdoor construction of the party, as far as tables and chairs and design were concerned. It was Dylan's wife, the lady of the mansion, Mrs. Sullivan, who had creative control of what the party would *look* like. But it was up to Owen to put it together for her.

He was given a crew of men to create whatever the woman had on her mind.

"Owen, you know how I feel about that. We have to have it outside."

Owen didn't want to argue with his boss. The almanac was right, and the storm was coming. He was sure of that.

But Dylan and Mattie were putting on an elaborate birthday party for their "almost five" son, Peter, whom everyone called Muddy. Muddy was well-spoken for an almost five-year-old. But despite the intelligence he seemed to have, he made terrible decisions. He had nearly died several times already from going places he knew he was not allowed, nearly being trampled by a bull. He'd even fallen down several holes, requiring great skill and good fortune to get him out.

They had taken him to the doctor that morning, but Owen didn't feel it was his place to ask for the results of the tests. He would find out through the murmurings of the staff anyway. If he thought it was appropriate, he would ask Sophia, the beautiful nanny,

Owen was a confident man, but Sophia stripped him of that confidence. He didn't know if he would ever have the nerve to speak to her. Not about anything in-depth, anyway.

The party was for Muddy. Because he was a beloved child, Owen understood that. But as beloved as the child was, the storm would not be stopped.

"I think it would be a good idea to have a backup plan. That's all I'm saying," Owen continued. "We can make sure one of the rooms is available for dancing, and we'll have decorations ready, and all the fun and games can be moved inside. I think that's a good idea, don't you?"

Dylan looked thoughtful, if not a little skeptical.

"Muddy really wants the party to be outside," he said. Owen was taken aback by how wounded the man sounded. It was as if the man felt he would be hurting his child if he didn't do what Muddy requested.

Owen's heartstrings were pulled. "I'll simply make a layout, sir. I'll have the men ready just in case. We have another few days to worry about it, right?"

"Maybe your almanac will be wrong this year." Even Dylan sounded doubtful when he said those words.

Owen didn't bother to respond. There was no need to point out that the almanac hadn't been wrong in years. And if it was, by now, Owen would be able to tell just by the feel of the air around him. It was damp a certain way before a big storm came, and Owen could feel it up to two days before the actual weather hit. It was a ability he'd discovered as a young man and had nurtured.

"Maybe it will be." Dylan sounded so young when he spoke, turning away from Owen. "Byron. Byron, over here."

Owen leaned forward slightly, hooking his thumbs in his belt and looking around his boss at his best friend, who was approaching on horseback.

"Howdy," Byron greeted them, raising his hat briefly before plopping it back on his head. "What are you two up to? Look like your schemin' about something."

Dylan let out a sharp laugh that made Owen glance over at him. "Your friend here is trying to convince me we should move the party inside again," he said.

Owen felt bad and had to jump to his own defense. "Now, that's not what I was saying, boss. I was just sayin' we should have a backup plan, that's all. A simple thing, not too much need to go into it."

He thought a lot would need to go into planning an indoor party as well as an outdoor party, but why mention it? He wasn't going to convince them a storm was coming. They didn't know his skill.

"I'm joking with you, Owen," Dylan retorted, giving him a big grin. Owen smiled back.

"All right, all right."

"Come on, Owen," Byron said, sliding out of his saddle, his blue eyes twinkling. "Stop bothering the man, and let's get to settin' up some tables."

"Way too early for that," Owen replied, jogging down the steps toward his friend.

"You two let me know about the chicken run," Dylan called out as he spun on one heel and headed for the door.

"Hey, what?" Both Owen and Byron yelled, but

Dylan didn't turn around. They looked at each other in bewilderment.

"What chicken run is he talking about?" Byron asked. "He say somethin' about that to you?"

Owen shook his head. "Not me. That man. Bet a buck he was messin' with us. Wants us confused. Come on." He tapped his friend on the chest with his knuckles. "Let's find somethin' to do."

3

Sophia carried Collin in her arms, walking around with Lydia—her best friend and the woman she had come to Bighorn with several years ago—and Mattie, the mother of her charges. Felix and Muddy were both with Lucy. They'd gone on a picnic near the pretty white bridge with blue trim that arched over the stream curling around the back of the Holbrook property.

It was by far the most luxurious residence and landscape Sophia had ever seen. It stretched on for what seemed like an eternity before the mountain was reached, and all of the back area was land-scaped so beautifully it made Sophia think of an oasis. At night there was a myriad of lamps on posts.

One of the boys from Bighorn was paid handsomely to walk the property from dusk until dawn, making sure the lamps were all lit and putting them out at daybreak.

Poachers, would-be thieves, and other ruffians were disposed of by Owen and the other ranch hands that acted as guards for the property as well as staff.

Lydia and Mattie were talking about the decorations. They weren't leaving Sophia out, but she found herself not really paying attention to what they were saying anyway. It wasn't a matter of station. Even though she was the nanny to the children, Mattie and Dylan treated her as one of their own, one of the wealthy people of station.

Not that they were much different from anyone else on their staff. They treated everyone with respect, which was sometimes hard to find when looking for employment. Sophia could remember other employers she'd had who weren't as respectful toward their staff.

"What do you think, Sophia?"

Alas, Lydia turned to her and asked the fateful question when she had no earthly idea what they'd been talking about.

"I... I'm sorry. My mind was a million miles away."

"Oh, I'm not surprised," Mattie said, shaking her head and looking at Lydia. "We've been walking in front of her, not including her all this time. She must be terribly upset with us both."

Sophia gave Mattie an affectionate glance, lifting her lips in a grin. "Don't be silly. I was truly thinking about something else. Please do repeat what you were saying, and I'll tell you what I think."

Lydia, who knew Sophia better than their friend Mattie, gave Sophia a look she recognized. Their friendship was strong. They knew each other so well. She felt a flood of fondness for Lydia fill her to the brim.

"I was suggesting Japanese lanterns to hang from the trees here and here. Well, starting here, I suppose, and going to there and there and there." As she spoke, Lydia pointed to various trees and areas where she thought the line of lanterns would look good. "And we can put the little tiny candles in each one."

"We could even pay the boy who watches the lamps at night to take care of them for us," Mattie added in an excited voice.

Lydia looked at the woman with amusement in her eyes. "So you've decided it's a good idea, then?"

"I like it," Sophia put in her opinion, imagining what the back courtyard would look like after it was all said and done. She wasn't quite sure where the games and booths and tables of food and drink were going, but she could imagine it.

As soon as the thought entered her mind, Sophia looked to her left and saw a ranch hand talking to Byron. She knew Byron. He'd been working for Dylan almost as long as she had. But the other one was new.

He'd been there a few months—Sophia wasn't sure exactly how long. She'd been admiring him from afar since the first time she laid eyes on him. She knew his name but rarely thought it. It made her feel a certain way, and she was afraid of that feeling.

"There's Owen and Byron," Mattie said, her voice lilting slightly. "Let's see what they've got planned. I know it's going to be good. Owen's plans are always good. Did you see that event he put together for the Codswolds last year? I was so envious."

Lydia nodded vigorously. "Yes. He's got an amazing talent. I'm sure he's going to make this incredible too. Muddy will be so happy."

"Owen. Owen!"

Sophia was about to die inside. Every time Mattie and Lydia said his name, she felt a little tingle, a twinge of excitement she didn't want to feel. And now Mattie was calling him over.

She was about to lose her nerve. She concentrated on the fact that she was holding Collin. She realized she was squeezing him when he wheezed and gave a soft cry that made her relax her grip.

Mattie, hearing the cry of her tiny son, reached for him without thinking. Sophia thought it was funny when the woman didn't move her eyes from Owen and even called out to him to make sure he knew she was speaking to him, all the while wrestling her son from Sophia's arms and pulling him into hers.

Sophia didn't mind a bit and only made sure the baby was safe with his mother before she completely let go. Collin gave her one of his sweet baby grins, filling Sophia's heart with warmth.

"Yoo hoo! Owen. Over here."

Sophia allowed herself to turn her eyes and take in the sight of Owen and Byron as the two men approached. Her heart went into overdrive, and she was almost uncomfortable with the feelings she was having. She didn't like not being in control. When

Owen was near, she felt like her tongue was tied, and her brain went blank.

Fortunately, this time, she wasn't required to say anything, so she could stand there and stare with a smile and not have to worry about thinking.

"Howdy," both men said at the same time. They approached, removing their hats from their heads at the same time as well.

Sophia was impressed by them both.

But mostly Owen.

"We were just talking about the party," Mattie said, "and I was wondering if you had any ideas you wanted to run by me since we are all here right now. Of course you know anything we need to take care of will be done quickly, but you have to tell us what you need, don't you?"

Owen's smile was so attractive it was hard for Sophia to look away. She hoped her cheeks weren't as red as she felt like they probably were. It was the sun. It was making her hot. That's what she would tell them if they asked.

They weren't going to ask, though. They weren't even looking at her.

"We were just talkin' about that, too," Byron remarked. "I think you're gonna like the layout and design me and Owen got goin' on right now. We'll put it on paper for ya if ya want. But we have to get some paper and ink to do that."

"That's something we've got in great supply," Mattie said with a laugh. The rest of them joined her, as it was common knowledge that Dylan was part owner of a magazine printing press.

"Soon as we get our hands on some paper, I'll draw you out a design," Owen continued.

At that moment, he turned his hazel eyes and looked directly at her.

Much to her utter dismay, Sophia's knees weakened, and she nearly tumbled to the ground. It was Byron who was closer to her, though, and he reached out a hand to steady her.

She took hold of it and righted herself, looking down at her feet in an accusatory way.

"Oh, my, excuse me," she stammered. "I... must be a little tired. I don't know what just happened."

When she was brave enough to lift her eyes again and look at Owen, all she saw in his returned gaze was concern.

"Are you all right?" he asked.

She nodded, her cheeks hot once more. "I am very embarrassed, but otherwise, I will be fine."

They all smiled, but it was his that warmed her heart and reinvigorated her confidence in herself.

"It's okay," he said. "We all nearly fall down sometimes."

His words were so casual they created another round of laughter, this time one that Sophia felt wonderful participating in.

4

"So we need to discuss the wine situation," Mattie said, drawing Owen's attention back to the conversation. He'd been caught up thinking about the beautiful nanny's near-fall and wasn't really paying attention as Mattie, Lydia, and Byron continued the conversation. He turned his eyes to her, feeling a bit of pain as he dragged his gaze from Sophia.

"What's wrong with the wine?" he asked curiously.

"I don't know how much we have," Mattie stated as if it was the end of the world. "I don't know what kind or how much or anything."

Owen had to frown, not understanding that at

all. "Why don't you know?" he asked. "It seems like something someone would know."

It seemed only logical to him. He dared a glance at the nanny, and she seemed as bewildered as him. In fact, Lydia and Byron did, too.

"I think someone needs to go down there and check it," Mattie said, narrowing her eyes at Owen. "You and Sophia should go and check the wine for me. You don't mind, do you?"

Owen's heart skipped a beat when he realized what it appeared Mattie was doing. His eyes darted to Sophia's face.

She was staring at her boss in astonishment. "I don't know anything about—"

"Balderdash." It was Lydia who broke into Sophia's statement. "I told Mattie what you did for me back in Virginia and how you knew all about the wine in the cellar while working for me. You are a connoisseur of sorts, and you know it."

Sophia flushed once more. Owen wondered how many times the woman was going to turn red in his presence. He didn't care. He thought she was beautiful no matter what state of flustered she was in.

"I guess I do know a thing or two about wine," she said meekly.

"You do, and you know it. And I'm sure Owen will be glad to help you with the counting and any heavy lifting you might need to do." Lydia turned her eyes to Owen. His heart jumped in his chest. "Won't you?"

He blinked rapidly. "Of course," he stated plainly.

"Well…" Sophia's eyes returned to his face. "All right. That's fine. But I will need a notepad and a pen."

"Not a problem. Sophia, you go on into Dylan's study and get whatever you need. I would like that done as soon as you can, please." Mattie looked from one to the other. "Now would be good."

Sophia giggled, and Owen raised his eyebrows at her. "Shall we?" he asked, lifting one arm and holding it toward the large house behind them.

"Most assuredly," Sophia responded in an excited voice. He hoped that was because they were finally going to get some time to talk. He couldn't think of any other reason for her to be excited. Unless she just really liked wine a lot.

He held the door open for her, and she passed him with a smile. It washed him over with an emotion he was getting very fond of.

She was quiet as they walked through the house. She didn't say anything until they reached the door of the study. What she did say when she spoke surprised him and gave him the impression she was at least a little interested in him. Maybe she had been for a while now.

"Do you mind if I ask why you left the Codswolds? Aren't they a good family?"

A flash of memories flooded Owen's mind just as warmth spread through his body, thinking about the family he'd worked for before the Sullivans and Holbrooks.

"Oh, yes, yes," he replied enthusiastically. "A good family, really. I guess it's just that I tend to move around a lot. I don't know when that's going to change. I've only left one place of employment because I didn't like it there, and that was when I was a teenager. I'm almost thirty now. I think about my future more now than I did back then."

"I understand what you mean. I've been looking for a sense of purpose since my mother died some years back. It's why I spent so many years as a companion for wealthy young ladies. I did that for seven years, from the time I was fourteen years old until I came to work here as a nanny."

Owen was astounded, and pleased Sophia was opening up so easily to him. "And do you like being in the company of children more than adults? Or the other way around?"

Sophia gave him an interesting look as she crossed the room to their boss's desk. She opened the middle drawer and took out a small pad of paper along with a pencil next to it. She held the pencil up and studied the end of it. He could see from where he was that it was sharp and ready to be used.

A smile of satisfaction lit Sophia's face. Owen wondered if she could possibly get any prettier than she was. He was constantly surprised by how attracted he was to her.

"Dylan always keeps his supplies in good order," she stated proudly as if he was *her* husband.

"You like working here, don't you?"

She nodded as she came back over to him. "Dylan and Mattie are wonderful. I still get to see Lydia, to whom I was a companion before, and I get to have adult interaction nearly as often as I do with the children. Mattie is a very involved mother, you know. She doesn't go a day without seeing the children. That isn't something that would even happen. She spends half her days with her children and the other half on herself. She is a very well-balanced woman."

"And the boys all know their mother loves them," Owen said, pulling the door closed after she came out to stand in the hallway with him.

She nodded. "Yes, that is exactly right. And she doesn't get troubled having to care for all three of them all the time. They are happy little boys, and that's all that matters."

Owen gave her a big smile. "You think they'd like to have a girl?"

Sophia's eyes lifted, and she appeared to think about it for a moment. "You know, I would just bet they do. But I don't know. I've never asked, and Mattie has never spoken about it."

"I'll bet they do, too," Owen responded. He turned his head and looked up and down the hallway they were standing in. "I... don't know how to get to the cellar. I've never been down there."

"I've got the key." Sophia pulled a small ring from the pocket of her white apron and held it up. There were several keys attached to it, which was more than Owen expected. He didn't ask where the other keys went to. His business was rarely inside the house, and if they felt he needed keys, they would give him some.

"Lead on, my lady," he said dramatically, sweeping his hand down the hallway. She grinned at him and pointed in the other direction.

"It's that way," she said in a sheepish voice.

He laughed softly and changed direction, sweeping his arm out once more.

"Lead on, my lady," he repeated.

She giggled and led him to the last door on the right at the end of the hall toward the back of the house. It was directly across from the door that went into the kitchen.

"There's a lantern right on the inside of the door there," Sophia said, pointing around him when he pulled the door open. He stared down into the darkness.

"It's a good thing. We'd break our necks in the darkness."

"Silly man. Of course there's light. Here, I'll get it."

Owen took a step back but kept a good eye on her to make sure she didn't trip and plummet down the steep steps into the darkness, probably breaking every bone in her body. She retrieved the lantern and soon had it lit.

"You ready?" she asked in an ominous voice,

holding the lantern up in front of her and making a spooky face.

"Oh, go on. Lunatic."

They both laughed as she turned and held out the lantern, going carefully down the steps.

5

———

The cellar was as dark as Sophia expected it to be. And so very quiet. She felt like she could hear her breath coming and going echoing on the walls around them. She could feel the dampness down to her very bones.

"It's a little scary down here," she whispered. Sure enough, she distinctly heard the whisper echo back to her. She glanced over her shoulder, holding the lantern up so she could see his face better. He was smiling at her. She marveled at how handsome he was. "I'm so glad you're with me. I wouldn't want to do this alone."

His expression was reassuring as he said, "There's nothing to fear down here, Sophia. It's just a wine cellar. That's what's down here. Wine."

"What if someone were lurking in the shadows, ready to pounce on us?"

Owen's laugh was confident and made her feel better, which surprised her at the same time. It wasn't a condescending laugh. It was pleasant and sweet. "My lady, I will protect you with my mighty sword and shield from whatever imaginary dragons enter your mind. We're safe. Don't you worry."

Sophia did feel better. She turned back to scan the long shelves that ran from one side of the room to the other. It wasn't just the one. There were rows of them, four in total. The wine wasn't the only thing being stored in the cellar. There were sacks of various foodstuffs, like flour and sugar.

Sophia had never seen such a hoard of food.

"My goodness," she murmured. "They are prepared, aren't they?"

"Probably had something to do with the war. Back then, this house was in the middle of a trail followed by several army units from both sides of the fighting. At any moment, the war could have come straight to this front door. The family living here then was determined not to be pushed out. So they prepared by getting as much food as they could and storing it down here."

Sophia nodded, interested in the tidbit of history.

"But wouldn't this food have attracted critters? And shouldn't it all have gone bad by now? Surely flour doesn't stay good forever."

"I don't honestly know the life of a sack of flour," Owen admitted in a sheepish voice that made Sophia's heart flip over, "but I do know that the Sullivans continued the tradition when Dylan's father bought the ranch."

"Well, I'll be. It seems you do know much more than I do. I wonder how that could be?" She tilted her head to the side, casting an admiring glance his way. "It seems you are more talkative than you look."

They were quiet for a moment, looking up at the wine bottles. Each walked down an aisle, running fingers over the dirt to reveal what the bottles contained.

"I am surprised they didn't come down here and dust regularly. It does look like someone has taken care of other parts of the cellar. Why not the wine bottles?"

Owen was examining a bottle on the end of the aisle she was standing in. "I really don't know," he murmured. "Maybe it gives them an appearance of being even older than they really are. Maybe it discourages stealing because no one can tell what's in the bottle they are getting." He grinned. "I don't suppose they would want to get a sniff of brandy when they were expecting gin, would they? Not a pleasant surprise."

Sophia giggled. "I take it you don't like brandy." She liked the way his eyes twinkled when he looked at her. He reached up and hooked his lantern on a nail sticking out of the wooden shelf at the top. "Not even a little bit," he replied. Did I make it that obvious?"

"Only a little bit," she replied. "Okay, let's start taking this inventory. What are we doing here?"

"Get out your pen and paper," Owen instructed. "I'll count the bottles and tell you what they are. You write it all down. Mattie said I could help with the heavy lifting, but she didn't say which wines or liquors she wanted us to bring up for the party."

"Do you suppose she wants us to use our own judgment? She said you're a connoisseur. So you know what is good and what isn't."

"Even experts have their own tastes," Sophia replied, "but I think I know her and the others well enough to know what they'll want with their steaks and seafood dinners. Do you see any burgundy? That's a nice one I think they will like. And we'll have a white wine, too."

"We'll have to take up a lot of bottles," Owen

said, scanning the shelves. "You want me to go through each of these until I find what you're looking for? You realize that will take forever, don't you? We won't have any time to talk and get to know each other."

The words that came out of Sophia's mouth right then stunned her and probably surprised Owen, too, though he didn't show it.

"Well, then, we will have to have lunch together after so we can do just that."

The two stood in silence for a moment, staring at each other. Sophia would have been embarrassed, but the look on his face was so sweet and compassionate. It made her want to grab his cheeks and kiss him firmly on the mouth.

"I think I'd like to have lunch with you, Sophia. I've been noticing you lately as if you were supposed to be put in my vision repeatedly. I've always wanted to talk to you. I just never had the time and kind of realized you didn't either."

"I do have time," Sophia said softly, not taking her eyes from the man. "I make time for the important things, always."

Sophia studied his face, noticing the twitch just subtly that told her he was elated to hear what she was saying.

"And you consider me to be one of those important things?"

Sophia kept her eyes on his. "I do," she replied, keeping her voice low. "I hope that's okay. I realize we hardly even met before. Certainly never spent any one-on-one time in the house."

"I hope that changes," Owen replied. "I'd really like to get to know you better."

"Let's make a plan." Sophia flipped the notepad to a clean sheet and wrote her name. She wrote his name underneath and looked up at him. "I'll be free after five today. Mattie and Dylan are taking the children to see Luke and his family for the night. A pre-party party, Mattie said. Izzie wants to have something for Muddy, too. So I'm off the hook tonight, and so is the rest of the staff. As long as their work is done."

Owen grinned. "Of course. All right, my lady, let's start getting these wine bottles sorted. I'll start on this end, and you start on that end. I'll call out when I get one that you suggested, and you write it down. You don't have to tell me when you find one. Then when we're done with that, we will write the ones we have that aren't those. In case she wants them. And we'll have dinner tonight. If that is okay with you?"

Sophia's heart pounded so hard in her chest that she thought it might come out of her chest.

"I would like that very much, Owen. Very much. Thank you for asking me."

The work would go quickly from that point on. Sophia and Owen inventoried with quiet efficiency.

Sophia caught the quick glances he sent her way, locking them away in her memory.

6

"Can I ask you a question?" Sophia asked, picking up her fork when a salad was placed before her. She scanned the ingredients before her, lettuce, cucumber, cheese, bits of hard-boiled egg, little round tomatoes... Her stomach grumbled. She wondered how he could afford such a meal on the salary he received from the Sullivans.

"Of course," he replied, digging into his own salad. "I will answer if I know the answer."

"Well, it is a little bit personal." Sophia hoped her voice didn't wobble when she spoke. She was usually so confident and strong. Being around Owen made her feel like a *woman*. Typically, she didn't even think about such things. Suddenly, she was concerned about what she was wearing and how her hair looked. These were never things she had worried about before.

She'd picked her favorite dress to wear tonight. The neckline swooped from one shoulder to the other, showing off her collarbone in a way that none of her other dresses did. She had on the pearl necklace her mother had left her. She fingered it nervously.

"I was wondering... how you can afford to bring me here. When you picked me up, I expected us to go to Petey's Diner. This..." She looked around at the luxurious room they were in. A dozen tables with four chairs each, several of them occupied. "This is so fancy. I could never afford anything like this. And the Sullivans pay me quite well."

He grinned, and it looked so boyish to Sophia, it tugged on her heartstrings.

"I have money from my family. We are well-off, I suppose you could say."

"So you don't need to be working at all?"

Owen shook his head. "My family owns one of the oil rigs in South Texas that has recently..." He chuckled. "... struck gold, I reckon you could say. We are not in need of money. I take these odd jobs because I want to."

"Will you tell me about yourself?" Sophia tilted her head to the side. She blinked at him, smiling.

"What do you want to know?" Owen asked, stabbing several ingredients on his plate and gazing at her with a contemplative look while he chewed.

Sophia's insides were tied in knots. That wasn't her usual reaction to a flirting man. Owen seemed so casual in his actions. How could he not be nervous? Was he really that confident in himself?

She pushed away her nervousness. What was she thinking? He was a man who was as secure in himself as she was in herself. Why hide her natural personality?

She pulled in a deep breath, squared her shoulders, and leaned toward him, batting her eyelashes gently. "I want to know everything. Do you still have your parents? Do you have brothers and sisters? Do you like working for the Sullivans? It sounds like you don't have to, so I'm assuming you must enjoy it. And I'm sure you don't have a woman in your life."

Owen shook his head, answering the last statement first before addressing the others. It was what she expected, and she was delighted when he fell gently into her trap.

"No, there is no woman in my life other than the one paying my salary and the one sitting across from me. As for the rest, I will gladly tell you my life story if you tell me yours."

"Mine is not very glamorous," Sophia responded, dropping her eyes to her plate. Her lettuce would be wilted before she got around to it. She got a good forkful and put it in her mouth. She realized she would have to take a few minutes to chew, so she did so quickly, noticing the amused look on Owen's face as he slowly at his own salad.

Sophia enjoyed the humor in his eyes. He smiled at the look on her face.

"So I'll tell you first since you're obviously pretty hungry."

Sophia almost choked and covered her mouth to let out a quick laugh. "Okay," she said quickly.

"I have a mother and a father, but my father died a few years ago. He had a heart attack. He'd always had some trouble with the old ticker."

"I'm so sorry to hear that," Sophia said, quickly swallowing so she could express her condolences.

Owen nodded. "Thanks. I loved the old man a lot. He made me the man I am today. I'm just grateful he led a good life and was well-loved by all. He had a lot of friends. He used to tell me his life was a series of misadventures from the beginning, and the only good stable thing in his whole existence was my mother and me. He loved us a lot, and we loved him, too. I have no doubt he's in Heaven having a wonderful time, and we'll see him again."

"That's so wonderful."

"Being in the oil business took my father around Texas, and he made a lot of friends. He was a naturally friendly man."

"Like you," Sophia injected. She couldn't believe she said it aloud moments after it was out.

His mouth was closed, but the corners of his lips lifted delightedly.

"I reckon," he said quietly. "Anyway, I didn't know how right he was until after he passed. That was when I had to take over some of the family business and start making some decisions on the oil rig. I'd always thought that was how we made our money. But for more than a decade, the rig lay dormant, unable to find oil. Through those years, the family was kept afloat by an invention of my father's that makes the harness on a horse bridle safer and more secure. It's just a small adjustment but adding the gadget allows the horses to pull more weight without strain on their bodies."

Sophia was impressed. She was sure the look on her face revealed as much.

"Well, I'll be," she murmured.

Owen nodded. "That's a typical response."

"So you grew up with your father gone a lot, but you didn't need any money?"

"Quite the contrary on the first part. Despite the work pa put into the oil rig and finding the perfect place to drill, he was at home a lot more than you might have thought. We had family dinners around the table often, at least four nights a week."

"That's wonderful to hear," Sophia gushed. "I also had a childhood where I was shown attention and love."

Owen sat forward, leaning over the table. "Maybe that's why we're both confident people who aren't afraid to be a little bold sometimes."

Sophia liked the sound of that. She was sure that if she and Owen didn't end up a couple, they would be great friends. She leaned closer.

"So, what do you want to do with your life, Owen? Will you be seeking adventure the way your father was?"

With every passing moment of the two of them so close to each other, Sophia's heart beat harder. Her nerves tingled like her skin, the hair standing up on end. She was very aware of his presence so close to hers.

She couldn't help wondering if he was feeling the same way as her, if the confidence he portrayed was real, and if he was waiting for her to make the next move.

Did she dare?

She practically melted inside when he answered, not moving away from her, using a warm, affectionate voice.

"I do want to explore. I don't know what or where but I have a... I feel a pull toward it. To walk, you know... seek out what the world can give me. Travel around."

"Did your pa do a lot of traveling?"

"Not really. Not once he had a family. He might have before. I wouldn't put it past him."

"I think if he'd traveled, he would have told you."

When Owen shook his head, Sophia wondered why she was talking to him about his pa when it was obviously a sensitive subject. She wished they'd never gotten on the topic.

"I don't know. Sometimes I don't think I knew the man at all."

"Tell me about your mother instead," Sophia prompted, not wanting the topic of conversation to ruin the evening but also reluctant to push away when answers were needed.

She could tell he was relieved by the inquiry into his mother. She would let him direct the conversation from now on. She didn't want to upset him.

7
———

Sophia didn't get home until well after dark. They'd almost closed down the restaurant. By the time she left the place, it felt like she'd known him for years. She didn't know if that was Mattie's intention to begin with, but if it was, she definitely had something to thank the woman for.

"Look at you, glowing and everything," Lucy was teasing her, giggling behind her hand.

Sophia felt her cheeks burn. "I'm not glowing," she said. "Don't be silly." She concentrated on changing the baby's nappy. "Get me that lotion there, would you?"

Lucy continued to giggle as she crossed the room to get the lotion. Collin didn't really need it, but Sophia had to do something to distract the woman.

"If you weren't falling for that man, you wouldn't be blushing like you are right now," Lucy continued, handing her the bottle.

Sophia snatched it from her friend. "Oh, stop it. You're embarrassing me."

"You shouldn't be." Lucy's voice was firm when she spoke that time. It got Sophia's attention. She gave the maid a curious glance. Lucy answered that with an exasperated expression. "Sophia, Owen is a good catch. He's a good man from all I've heard. And I haven't heard a lot, either, which is good sometimes. Anything I did hear has been good, and you would do well not to turn him away. He could give you a happy life."

For a moment, Sophia wondered what made Lucy think she didn't already have a happy life. She didn't pursue that line of thinking, though, because she didn't believe that was Lucy's intention.

"I am not turning him away, Lucy," she said, a lilt in her voice to show she was not upset by the conversation. "I am... interested in Owen. I would like to see him again, and I am sure he knows that. We had a wonderful time at dinner. I would like to do that again."

"Do you think he will ask you?"

Sophia pulled in a deep breath, securing the baby's diaper around him and lifting him, so he was on his feet. He wobbled for a moment and then plopped down on his behind. His eyes widened, and his arms lifted, but he looked up at Sophia and laughed delightedly. It was a game he liked to play, and she knew it. Someday she would put him on his feet, and he would stay there, wondering what happened to the sitting game.

But for now, he wasn't yet standing or walking, so he liked the sitting game. She gently lifted him to his feet again and took her hands away, watching closely. She wouldn't let him be hurt, but she didn't want to deprive him of something he thought was fun.

He wobbled a second and plopped down, laughing again.

"I do think he will," she responded to Lucy's inquiry. "But for now, the party is most important. Muddy has to be spoiled, spoiled, spoiled for his birthday." Sophia said the words with great affection, grinning wide at Muddy, who was on his belly near her, playing with wooden horses, which he trotted across the floor majestically.

He wasn't looking at her, and it was doubtful he'd heard her words or understood them if he did.

She averted her eyes to Lucy, and both women chuckled.

"He will be, but if there was ever a boy who deserved it, it's that one. So precocious and smart."

"Yeah, he is, isn't he?"

Sophia played the sitting game with Collin twice more before the baby was tired of it. The last time she put him on his feet and he sat down, he just giggled slightly, turned over, and crawled away from her toward a large box filled with toys.

Sophia watched him. For the first time in a very long time, she wondered what it would be like to have her own children. She'd stopped thinking about that possibility when she'd entered the employment of Kenneth Green, whose wife she was to be a companion to. It was that misadventure that had brought her here to Bighorn, Texas four years ago, and she would never be happier that she'd decided to stay.

Sophia hadn't really entertained the thought of children more than a smidgen anyway. She had never had a long-term beau and had never had the prospect of marriage on the table. As a young girl, she'd expected to get married and have children, but the opportunity had never presented itself.

Not until now.

It wasn't that she hadn't fallen in love before. This was the first time as an adult, though, and with a man who seemed to show the same mature interest in her that she had in him. It wasn't about how good-looking he was or how bubbly he made her feel inside.

That was *part* of it. It just wasn't *all* of it, like it had been when she was an infatuated teenager.

The door opened behind her, and she twisted as she pushed to her feet. It was Dennis, the butler. He smiled at both, sweeping his bright blue eyes around the room to take in all the little faces as well. He was a rather large man with a mop of unruly blond hair on his head and the most contagious smile of anyone Sophia had ever met.

"And how is everyone in the nursery today?" he asked in an overly-excited voice.

"Denny," cried Muddy, leaping to his feet and running toward the large man to jump into his arms.

"Hello, little Muddy-man," Dennis said. "You behave like you haven't seen me for a year."

"It *has* been a year," Muddy exclaimed seriously, giving the man a stern look before throwing his arms around Dennis' neck.

Collin couldn't run to Dennis the way Muddy had, but Felix wobbled over, showing as much elation as his older brother had. Collin just clapped his hands and laughed when Dennis trotted over and scooped the baby up off the floor. Felix had wrapped his arms and legs around Dennis' right leg and was holding on for dear life.

"Den-den," Felix cried out happily.

"Look at these little men," Dennis gushed as if showing them to the ladies for the first time. "Aren't they the brightest little men on the planet?"

"They are," Lucy and Sophia replied dutifully, both grinning from ear to ear.

"I thought I'd come in here and sweep up some little kiddos, relax a little bit. The folks have gone out, and we're in charge of the household for a couple of hours. Nothing like a little vacation while the folks are gone, right, kiddo?" He was holding Collin up in the air with one hand, his fingers splayed out, clutching the baby. He brought the little boy directly to his face, so they were touching noses, widening his eyes. "Right, kiddo?" he repeated in a silly voice, making Collin laugh.

"Sure sounds like a fun time for all," Lucy said, reaching to her left and grabbing a chair. She shoved it behind Dennis, and the big man dropped down in it.

Sophia was afraid for a moment that it would

snap in two or the legs would break under his weight, but it held up surprisingly well, especially since the boys were still climbing all over him.

She stood up when it looked like Dennis was struggling a bit.

"All right, boys," she called out, clapping her hands together. "You have to let the man breathe. Otherwise, he won't be able to play with you because he will be laid out on the floor unconscious. You don't want to do that to him, do you?"

"No. No," the three boys cried out at the same time.

Sophia couldn't help looking at Collin, who shouldn't have understood what she said. She surmised he was mimicking his brothers. When she averted her eyes to look at Lucy, she could tell by the look on the maid's face that she'd been thinking the same thing.

"Momma and Papa should be back very soon," Dennis said, giving Sophia a grateful look as he peeled Muddy's arms from around his shoulders while she pulled Felix from his leg. "I think you boys could do with a nice story. Would you like that?"

"Yes. Yes!" Muddy jumped up and down, clapping his hands while he answered with exuberance. Collin once again copied him, sitting up on the floor and clapping his hands together, calling out "Yes. Yes," just like Muddy.

Felix didn't respond, but Sophia almost fell out of her chair when he lifted one arm to prop on Dennis' large leg and gave him an expectant look.

Dennis met her eyes. "So cute," he said.

She couldn't have agreed more.

8

Owen swung the ax over his head and brought it down on the medium-sized log so that it split in half. Chopping wood was a laborious job, one of the few that Owen didn't care for. He didn't mind a bit of hard work. But he'd found the task to be difficult for him, causing him anguish when he was a younger man and had to do it as a chore for his parents.

He was going to do it regardless since the task had been assigned to him, but he wished he could get Byron to cut more of it.

Byron was the first friend he'd made when he came to work at the ranch. They had common interests and liked each other from the moment they met.

They also worked in sync, which made their tasks go by a lot faster.

Byron had already cut his fair share of wood, so Owen wasn't about to ask him if he'd do Owen's share as well. But the temptation to ask was still there.

Owen's thoughts amused him. He turned his head to see what Byron was doing, ready to make a snarky remark about how Byron was sitting while he was working his fingers to the bone. He didn't get the opportunity, though, because Byron was working around the barn, stacking wood so that it was under the overhang and wouldn't be in the way of people, horses, and wagons passing by on the dirt path.

"Look at you, always working. Startin' to make me look bad over here," Owen teased his friend, who gave him a confused look at first. Byron stepped out and over some debris, glancing down so he wouldn't trip.

"If you ain't working, it's you who's makin' yourself look bad," Byron replied. He actually had a great sense of humor. Owen knew he'd just caught his friend off-guard.

"If that ain't the truth," Owen responded, moving to pick up both pieces of wood on the tree trunk in front of him and tossing them over to where Byron was. "Stack those on there, too, wouldja?"

"Yeah, that's what I'm aimin' for."

Owen turned to get another large log from the stack behind him.

"So..."

Owen felt his heart thump in his chest. Just the sound of that word and the way it was spoken told Owen his friend was going to tease him about something. His first thought was Sophia. He didn't mind if Byron teased him about Sophia. She was on his mind anyway.

"How was that dinner of yours last night? I didn't get back until late, and you were already asleep."

Owen grinned, though he wasn't facing his friend. He continued to adjust the log on the tree trunk until it looked choppable. "It was great," he said enthusiastically. "I had a good time with her. I'm hopin' she'll want to do that again sometime. After the party, of course. After the storm that's gonna blow away all the decorations we put up."

Byron met his eyes when he glanced over at him. "You still think that's gonna happen?" Byron sounded skeptical. "The party is tomorrow. I don't see no clouds on the horizon."

Owen grunted. "You oughta know that doesn't

mean no storm is coming. I'm tellin' you the almanac is never wrong. We're all gonna get blown away. I wish he'd listened to me and did it early or put it off until the weekend. More people could come on the weekend anyway."

"I understand he wants to do it on the day of his kid's birth."

Owen raised the ax, leveled it, and brought it down on the wood, which neatly fell in two parts. He stepped forward to retrieve them. "I understand that. I really do. But Muddy wouldn't know or care. He wouldn't remember. He won't remember any of this at all. It's all for his folks, God love 'em. I'm not speakin' ill of them, I promise. I'm just sayin' he's four. Four. He won't know."

"He might," Byron said, a level of humor in his voice. "He's turning five, after all, and that's a big boy, ain't it?"

Owen laughed. "Yeah, I reckon if you ask him, he's definitely a big boy. But he still loves those mud puddles, and I'm tellin' you we're gonna have a whole lot of 'em come the day after tomorrow. We're choppin' up wood for nothin' if he plans to have a big outdoor fire, too."

"That's what he's planning," Byron confirmed, "but if there is a big storm, they're gonna be needing all this wood inside. So it won't go to waste."

"It will if it's already burnin' outside when the storm hits," Owen replied. "I don't wanna be a stick in the mud, no pun intended. I'm just sayin' I'd hate to see all this goin' to waste when I'm certain a storm is heading our way. A massive one that we won't be able to avoid."

"You've told that to Dylan, right?"

"Of course. And Mattie, too."

"Did they listen to you?"

"No, sir, they did not."

"Then what more can you do?" Byron caught the pieces of wood Owen threw to him and tossed them over his shoulder onto the unruly stack he was transferring to the ruly stack. "Only thing left for you to do is prepare for what's to come. If there is no storm, good for the Sullivans. If there is a storm, good for you for being prepared."

"I'm gonna have to get the cooperation of some of the household staff, though. I might have to go behind Dylan's back. And I only have one day to do it."

"That's a simple fix," Byron said, coming over to take the ax from Owen's hand. "I'll do it. I can tell you don't want to. You stack the wood instead."

Owen felt a sweep of relief. "Thank you, Byron. I appreciate that. So how is there a simple fix?"

Byron chopped the wood twice as fast as Owen was, keeping Owen catching the wood and stacking them behind him as he spoke.

"You gotta think like Dylan. He's got an entire ranch to run, but he doesn't do more than observe and delegate. He's got a housekeeper to take care of the inside of the house, so he and Mattie don't have to be constantly on top of everything. He's got Andrew, the foreman, to take care of delegating tasks to us, so we know what we have to do every day without bothering him about it. So you want help from the inside staff? Who do you talk to? The maid, Lucy?"

Owen shook his head, catching two pieces of wood from midair after they were flung toward him. "No. I'd go to Dennis. Or Florence. The butler or the housekeeper. One of them."

Byron nodded. "Exactly. And if I were you, I'd go to both of them, maybe tell them together what you're thinkin' is gonna happen. They need to have a room big enough for all the guests and enough food and fires burnin' to accommodate those who want to wait out the storm. They'll take care of that. We already know what's going on outside so we can get a couple of men to be ready in case we need to get any presents and the like inside. If his cake is outside, that's the first thing we need inside."

"Besides the people."

Byron chuckled. "Yeah. Exactly."

Owen liked his friend's suggestions. He nodded, neatly catching two more pieces of wood Byron tossed his way. "Thanks. That's what I'll do. I can get them to help. And I'll let Sophia know what's going on, too, so she can be watchful for people who are left behind or straggling for some reason."

"You've got a big heart, thinkin' the way you do, Owen," Byron said appreciatively, leveling another batch of wood toward his friend. "I'm actually glad ya got yer eye on the almanac and the weather. That's somethin' we should all be payin' attention to."

Owen smiled at Byron. "Just hopin' I'm right and don't end up lookin' foolish in front of the Sullivans and... everyone else."

Byron just chuckled.

9

———

Sophia glanced out the window as she passed and stopped abruptly, catching sight of Owen out by the barn with another ranch hand. They were laughing about something. The look of amusement on both the men's faces made Sophia grin. She wondered what they were talking about.

If she'd been any other woman, like Mattie perhaps—the mistress of the manor, so to speak, she would have boldly gone out and asked them to amuse her with whatever they were laughing about. Maybe it wouldn't have been funny to her. But she wouldn't care. She'd only go out there in the first place so she could spend a moment of time near Owen.

As it was, she was neither the mistress of the house nor Mattie, so she couldn't put her natural boldness into play. She had to rein it in and go about her business.

That didn't stop her from gazing at Owen for a bit longer. It's not like her own tasks were all that pressing. She enjoyed watching the men work and admired how expertly Owen caught the two halves of a log of wood that came flying at him every minute or two.

The other ranch hand, whom Sophia knew as Byron, stopped chopping and leaned the head of the ax on the tree trunk, holding the handle up toward the sky. He was talking to Owen, gesturing with his other hand.

Owen came out from under the awning that stretched out from the roof of the barn. He looked toward the sky and did some of his own gesturing.

His and Byron's actions made Sophia lift her teal-blue eyes to the sky as well. She'd heard a rumor that someone was saying a storm was coming. She wondered if it was Byron saying it or Owen. She didn't know what to believe. It certainly didn't look like the weather would turn bad.

"Lucy," she said, drawing the attention of the

maid, who was behind her working on needlepoint while the children took their afternoon naps. "Is there supposed to be a storm or not? Did you hear that someone was saying we needed to watch out for bad weather?"

"I heard. It was Owen that was telling Dylan that the other day. Word got around, but nobody is taking it seriously."

Sophia pulled her eyebrows together, thinking back to what she'd heard on the rumor mill. "The word is that the almanac was right the past few years, and it predicted a storm around this time of year."

"That's nothing," Lucy replied nonchalantly. Sophia looked over her shoulder at the young woman, whose eyes were still focused on her needlework. "There are always storms around this time of year. What are the chances it will come on the exact day of the year predicted in the almanac?"

"But it was right before. To the day." Sophia didn't want to argue, nor did she want to sound insistent about something she didn't really know. It did seem logical to her, though, that if it was right and someone was sure it would be right again, wasn't it better to err on the side of caution?

"I suppose Dylan and Mattie wouldn't change the date just in case." She didn't expect an answer from her friend. Lucy lifted her eyes from the sewing, lowering it to her lap. She gave Sophia a blank look.

"That wouldn't make sense," she said. "Then what if the storm happened on the date they changed it to? What if the actual day of Muddy's birth came and went without a storm? It would be Owen who would suffer for that. I'm sure Dylan has some plan to take care of everything if that happens. But I don't think it will."

Sophia wanted to say something else but kept her mouth shut. She didn't want Owen to get in trouble with their bosses. Why start a fuss with her friend when Lucy was right. There was nothing she could do about any of it.

She turned her head from Lucy, nodding so the woman would feel acknowledged. It worked as Lucy went back to her sewing.

She returned her eyes to the men in front of the barn. They were nearly done with the stack of wood they had gathered for cutting. She wondered what they would do if she went down there and offered to bring the wood in. There was a fire in her that had been lying dormant since she'd arrived in Bighorn.

There was no excitement on a day-to-day basis like there had been before. Her life had become peaceful and boring.

Owen coming into the picture, with his controversial ideas and eagerness to have them be heard, felt like a sure sign that her life would soon be exciting again. When that thought entered her mind, she felt a tingle of anticipation crawl up her spine.

Without speaking to Lucy, she went to the door of the nursery and pulled it open. She poked her head out and looked to the right toward the end of the hallway. The landing that led to the stairs to go down was lit up by a streak of sunlight coming in through the arched window behind it. It obscured the face of the grandfather clock she was trying to look at.

She left the door open to the nursery as she went down the hall a few feet until the light of the sun retreated from her vision. It was nearly four. She would be working into the evening, making sure the last-minute touches were put to the party set-up outside. Muddy had no idea what was going on. What four-year-old would?

It was definitely grand enough for a sixteen-year-old, but no one was going to complain. Everyone loved Muddy, who had taken the hearts of everyone in Bighorn by storm practically from the moment he was born. When he took his first step, everyone in the house had to stop what they were doing to come and watch. When he uttered his first word, the household staff spread the news around with joy, and there was dancing in the hallways. Dennis and the long-suffering housekeeper, Florence, had literally one a little jig down the hallway, making the other staff members laugh and clap.

Everyone loved Muddy. Sophia could understand why Owen wouldn't want to be the one to put a damper on the child's birthday party celebrations.

"Where did you go?" Lucy asked, crinkling her forehead in curiosity.

"Just checking the time," Sophia responded. "It's nearly four. Are you going to stay up here with the children while I finish off the rest of the list Mattie gave us earlier?"

"That's fine with me. Or you can stay up here with them."

"I'll do the work," Sophia replied hurriedly. Most of what she had to do would have her outside, which meant there was a good chance she would run into Owen along the way. Plus, Mattie was apparently going out of her way to pair them up. Sophia didn't have a problem with that at all.

She and Lucy nodded at each other, and she left the room.

It only took her a minute or so to get outside. She racked her brain, trying to think of something she needed to do that would take her toward the barn area. Most of the decorations were up. The booths had been built. The pen for the animal petting zoo had already been created and was waiting for the pets of the families attending the party. Dylan had made it a big thing for the children to know that they weren't the only ones invited—their pets were to come along and join in the fun, as well.

As she passed the makeshift pen, Sophia looked at its construction, wondering if it would hold out in a storm of the magnitude Owen was concerned about.

She slowed her pace as she got closer to the backside of the house, where the barn was closest. There were several tables there, ready and waiting for the guests to arrive. Only the decorations, plates, glasses, and utensils were on the table. The food wouldn't be brought out until the next day.

To her surprise, the men weren't where they had been minutes before.

Her excitement dashed to bits, Sophia halted in place and turned away, determined to focus her

mind on her work when there was so much that
needed to be done.

10

—————

Sophia had only had time to wave and smile at Owen the rest of that day. She slept peacefully, dreaming of a future she hoped would be hers. It included Owen. And several children who looked remarkably like them both. The Sullivan mansion had been their family home in her dream. Sophia was sure that was only because it had truly become her home since she came to be employed there.

She woke up refreshed and wide awake. She hopped out of bed and was finished with her regular morning duties in about twenty minutes. It was her job to get Collin and Felix ready for the party. Lucy had volunteered to keep an eye on the birthday boy.

All Sophia could think about the entire time

while she got the babies ready for the day was Owen. She changed both the boys into their day clothes, special ones since there would be a party, but also clothes she knew could still be played in without the Sullivans getting upset. There would be a lot of animals, games, and other children for both Collin and Felix to play with. She didn't want either of them to get in trouble or herself either.

They were in playful moods when she took them downstairs to the kitchen. They had a small table that was just for them to eat their breakfast at. It was fitted with a chair attached to the table so Collin could eat without falling over and would soon learn to feed himself by watching his brothers and others eat properly.

She stood at the window of the kitchen, watching as people arrived to take stations around the back of the Sullivan ranch. They had been hired just for the party, and Sophia only knew a few of them from around Bighorn. There would be a staff meeting before the party began. Guests weren't supposed to arrive for another five hours—starting around noon.

She was looking forward to the staff meeting. It was her goal to stand as close to Owen as she could get.

"Soooopphiiiieeee…" Felix got her attention by calling out her name and banging his spoon on the side of his bowl.

Sophia was immediately by his side to see what was the matter. He was just being silly, she discovered, when she asked him what was wrong and he had no answer.

"You just wanted my attention, didn't you, little man?" she asked, amused by his antics. She poked him in the neck to tickle him, and he jerked away laughing. "You go on and eat that food, young fella. Muddy will be down soon, and you know what? It is his birthday today. So you will have cake and cookies and lots of little friends to play with."

Felix was staring at her as she spoke, but she was fairly certain he didn't know what she was saying. He might have understood a few words, but for the most part, he was just gazing at her because she was talking. It was the same with Collin. And at least with him, she knew he had no idea at all what she might have been saying.

"You go on and eat your food," she prompted Felix again, returning him to the bowl of oatmeal in front of him. It hadn't taken her long to get the child to understand oatmeal was not to be eaten with fingers. Collin still had a ways to go before he would be doing anything like that on his own.

"Good practice for you, wouldn't you say?"

Sophia turned to see Dolly, the cook, behind her, grinning. She raised her eyebrows.

"I beg your pardon?" she asked.

Dolly chuckled, her large belly bouncing. "You are getting in practice for when you have your own," she reiterated. "I can tell. You are ready for your own family."

Sophia flushed, feeling her face turn hot. "I need a husband before I can have children to care for," she replied.

Dolly continued to laugh softly. "I see the eyes you make to that Owen they hired a few months back. Didn't you have dinner with him recently?"

Sophia's face felt even hotter. She turned back to the children and pretended to be helping them. "Yes. I had dinner with him a few nights back. It was the first time. We talked and had a good time together. That does not mean we will get married and have children."

What Dolly said next made Sophia feel warm inside.

"You're not the kind of woman to freely give her heart to just anyone, my dear. I've seen you with other men, other ranch hands that you've talked to and spent a little time with, and never have I seen you look as happy as you do now. Ever since you went to dinner with him, you've looked happier. You must feel it. If we can see it, you must be able to feel it."

She spoke with such confidence, in such a matter-of-fact way. Sophia was almost convinced of it herself. She certainly hoped it would go the way Dolly was saying it would.

"Well, we are still very early on in this relationship," she said hurriedly, "if that's what this is. And I don't want it to be rushed. I want to make sure it's the right thing for both of us before I make any decisions. I'm too old to be reckless about it."

"Too old?" Dolly laughed again. "You are twenty-five, isn't that right?"

"Yes. And getting older every day. Soon, men won't want me anymore." Sophia was purposefully being pouty, pushing out her lower lip and putting on a sad face. This only made Dolly laugh harder, as she could see through Sophia's amusing façade.

"That is not only a silly thing to say but won't even matter after you and Owen fall in love. Oh, I'm just glad I'm here to see it." The woman clapped help laughing herself.

"Done," Felix announced so loudly. Sophia saw baby Collin jump in his highchair and give his brother a stern look.

"All right, Felix, you just stay in your seat until your brother is finished with his breakfast. Then we'll go outside, and you can play in the field, all right?"

"Horses," Felix barked the word, banging his spoon on the table. "Horses. Horses!"

"I'll take you to see the horses, of course," Sophia told him while stripping him of the noise-making spoon. "You just stay right there, all right?"

She pulled a small wooden horse from the pocket of her apron and set it in front of him. "You can play with this until he's done. Play quietly. No whinnying too loudly now."

Felix did as he was told, pretending the horse was running and jumping along the side of the table while whinnying under his breath.

"You're going to be a good mother, you know," Dolly remarked, eyeing Sophia. She was helping Collin with the last of his oatmeal, spooning the food into his mouth at a rate he could handle. He wasn't a fast eater like his brother.

"Lucy should be down with Muddy in a few

minutes," Sophia told the cook. "Dylan said he could sleep in a whole hour today."

"And how did you draw the short straw?" Dolly asked, glancing at the two younger boys.

"Oh, I volunteered," Sophia answered her.

One side of Dolly's lips lifted in a knowing grin. "There was a certain ranch hand that you might be able to see if you're up earlier. Is that right?"

Sophia wrinkled her nose at the cook and stuck out the tip of her tongue. Just after she looked away, she mumbled, "Maybe."

Dolly laughed uproariously at that.

"All right, boys, all done," Sophia announced when Collin took his last bite of oatmeal. "Let's go get our shoes on so we can go outside and play. Come on, Felix. Time to go see the horsies."

"Horsies," Felix cried out. "Horsies."

"Yes, that's right. Come along. Shoes in the mudroom. Follow me." She waved to Felix, lifting Collin from his chair. She marched out of the kitchen, swinging the other arm dramatically and lifting her knees up as she went. Felix marched behind her in a similar fashion, pretending to be a military man.

11

———

Owen was the first person she saw coming around the corner of the house on the side where the bunkhouse and chow house were. There were several ranch hands that followed behind him, and there were probably more that had already come out to the party area. But he was the first one Sophia laid her eyes on.

The staff meeting was about to begin. She had taken a spot on the steps that created a huge half-circle against the back of the house. In the middle of the half-circle was the veranda that attached to the house. There were two sets of glass double doors letting out to the veranda. This was where the guests would come out. Some of the staff would be standing there to greet them and direct them to wherever they needed to go.

Most of the guests would probably be going to the animal "petting zoo" first to drop off their animals.

Owen noticed her and made a beeline toward her. She saw that his friend Byron was right behind him, saw where he was headed, and followed along.

"Good morning," Owen said when he was close enough.

"Good morning to you," Sophia responded. "How are you today?"

"I'm feeling good. Excited about the party." He turned his eyes to take in the sky in the distance, and Sophia did the same. "Looks like the almanac might have been wrong this year. Or maybe God's looking in favor upon the child, seeing as it is his birthday."

She saw nothing but clear blue as far as she could see. "Wouldn't that be nice? I think the almanac might have been wrong. I'm more inclined to think a man writing that would be wrong than God Himself."

"I think you're right about that," Owen replied with a laugh. "You know Byron, don't you?"

"Not formally." Sophia held out her hand. Byron looked impressed when he shook it.

"Nice to meet you," the tall man said, his dark eyes flashing at her.

"You, as well," she replied, letting her eyes linger on him only a moment more before returning them to Owen's handsome face.

"What's your job consist of today?" Owen asked, coming closer to stand right next to her, making her heart pound and sudden butterflies to go wild in her stomach.

"Oh..." She forced herself to be casual. "I'll be taking care of the two smaller babies. Collin here..." She gestured to the little boy in the rolling stroller next to her. "And Felix, who is currently at the petting zoo, watching all the new pets come in with his brother."

"Ah, the birthday boy."

Sophia grinned at him. "The one and only. So I've been given some free time, as Lucy is in charge of them while they're with her."

"Would you like to mingle with me when the party gets started?"

Sophia almost lost her breath when she asked him that question.

He continued as if he didn't notice he'd swept her right off her feet. "I'm the newest hire here, and Byron has his sister and her family coming, so he'll be with them. I'll be all alone." He said the last sentence, reducing his voice to one of a five-year-old, and stuck out his lower lip.

Sophia couldn't help laughing. "I don't want you to be unhappy at a party," she exclaimed. "I will gladly walk around with you. I know quite a few people here in Bighorn you might be interested in knowing."

Owen raised his eyebrows, giving her a curious look. "What do you mean?"

"Well, you don't have to do the work you're doing, correct?"

"That's right," he responded.

"So if you were to meet some of the wealthy people of Bighorn, you might find a profession that will allow you to settle down, but you'll still be happy with your life."

Owen kept his eyes locked on hers. Sophia felt like he was boring into her soul. "Are you saying it's time for me to settle down?"

Sophia hadn't realized that was her intention. But when he said it, she knew it was.

"It might be," she responded. "I mean, you're getting up in years. Soon you will be relying on someone else to take care of you."

He burst out laughing. "Sophia, I love your sense of humor." She was glad he recognized she was teasing him. "But you may have a point. I'm getting closer to thirty every year, aren't I? Maybe it is time I looked into finding a permanent home."

"Will you go back to your hometown where you grew up?" Sophia hoped not. She planned to encourage him strongly to stay right there in Bighorn and take advantage of all Texas had to offer.

"I don't think so. I've been to a lot of places and seen some wondrous sights. I think I like Texas the best. I'll stay here in this state. I know that."

Sophia wasn't too disappointed with that answer. She would just have to push for the best little city in Texas—Bighorn—until Owen couldn't imagine leaving. She looked down at the baby in the stroller. He was slumped to one side, his eyes closed, a little bubble of spittle around his tiny mouth. Sophia mopped it gently with a soft cloth.

When she stood up again, she glanced at Owen. The look on his face made her chest tighten. His face reminded her of Dylan's when he looked at Mattie while she was surrounded by their children. Sophia got the strong impression Owen was picturing her as his wife and Collin as their baby.

Her thoughts made Sophia feel hot. Suddenly, she was very thirsty. She straightened, looking toward the refreshments table.

"I... I think I need a drink," she said, feeling awkward for no reason.

"Well, that sounds like a mighty fine idea," Owen exclaimed. He held out one hand toward the table. "Shall we go over together, or would you like me to fetch a drink for you? I don't mind."

"We can go together," Sophia replied hurriedly. She didn't want to give Owen the impression she thought he was obligated to do anything for her. Her attraction to him was obvious enough. She pushed the stroller over the grass toward the table, sweeping her eyes over the area until she settled them on Felix and Muddy near the petting zoo.

She did let Owen make her a cup of lemonade, but only because all he had to do was pick up the premade cup from the table and hand it to her. "It probably hasn't gotten too warm yet," he said. "It might cool you down."

Sophia gave him a grateful smile before drinking half the cup down. The sweet and sour taste mixed in her mouth, reinvigorating her energy. She almost wished she didn't have to push the stroller around and could just freely wander around with Owen. But she wouldn't shirk her responsibilities, and it wasn't like Collin was difficult to care for.

"I talked to Lucy and Florence last night about

the…" Sophia stopped for a moment, trying to figure out the best words to use for what she wanted to say. She looked at him, and his eyebrows shot up curiously. "The storm warning?"

He nodded. "The storm that isn't coming after all?"

Sophia couldn't help glancing out at the horizon, but still, she saw nothing to cause her any alarm. "Yes, I suppose. We were planning to move everything indoors to the ballroom—or the entertainment room. Dylan had us move all the furniture and the piano and other things to the sides of the room in case we all needed to dash in here. And did you know Cook made two cakes, just in case?"

"Really." Owen shook his head. "I hope no one is upset with me for telling Dylan the storm might come and destroy the party. I didn't mean to cause more work for anyone."

"I think that was inevitable if we want to be cautious. And I think you were wise to give Dylan a warning. Better to know than be surprised."

Owen's smile was gratifying. It was nice, Sophia thought, to feel so comfortable with a man. She'd never felt that way before.

12

Owen had never attended a party like the one the Sullivans were throwing for their now-five-year-old child. Muddy appeared to be having the time of his life, and Owen had to give credit where it was due. Dylan and Mattie had planned the activities perfectly for both the children and the adults. He was particularly interested in the kissing booth and was glad Sophia wasn't behind the little table, offering a sweet kiss on the cheek—leaving, of course, the red lipstick mark just for fun. There were a growing number of little boys with red lips on their cheeks and silly grins on their faces.

A band played happy, jaunty tunes while people walked around, talking, sharing jokes, and playing fun games. It was the biggest birthday party Owen had ever seen.

"Owen!"

He heard Byron's voice calling from a distance and turned to see his friend jogging toward him. His smile quickly disappeared when he saw the look on the man's face.

"What's going on?" he asked, turning away from Sophia, who shared his concern.

"I just need your help fixing one of the games. It must have been old. The wood snapped."

Owen was surprised Byron wanted his help for something that sounded so easy. He suspected his friend was trying to get him away from Sophia for some reason. He hoped it was a good one because he didn't want to waste any time when he could be spending it with her. He gave her a puzzled look but said, "I'll be back soon. Don't go wandering off where I can't find you."

Sophia smiled, sending a warm feeling through Owen's body. "Oh, you'll spot me. I've got this big stroller with me, don't I?"

Owen glanced down at the sleeping baby. "True. Okay, show me what you need help with, Byron."

When the two men were a few feet away from

Sophia and other guests that were milling nearby, Owen looked over at Byron, raising his eyebrows.

"What's the real reason you wanted to talk to me?"

Byron pressed his lips together, only moving his eyes in his friend's direction, not really looking at him. "Can't fool you, can I?"

"I pride myself on my strong intuition. Now, what's the problem?"

Byron grimaced, turning sheepish eyes to his friend. "Bob got out."

Owen was washed over with a feeling of dread. He pictured the two thousand pound bull strolling into the back lawn and destroying everything in sight, including taking down a few guests.

"How did that happen?" he asked, his voice an octave higher than usual. It was strained and filled with tension. His eyes swept from side to side, searching for the massive beast.

"Something must have bothered him," Byron replied. He was now slightly behind Owen as they marched toward the cow pasture and bull barn. "It might have been another animal. A wild animal. I don't think it's because of the party. But I couldn't tell ya. I don't think like a bull, do I?"

"Where is he now?"

"He's in the cow pasture, circling around like he's looking for something to kill."

Owen let out a single chuckle, glancing over at his friend. "He's not looking for something to kill. He's an animal. He's just doing what comes naturally to him. Come on. I'm sure we can get him in and take care of this situation before anybody gets hurt. No need to let the guests know either."

Owen glanced over his shoulder before he went around the house. Sophia was standing in the same place and was still watching him. He turned back, a delighted feeling in his chest.

The bull was exactly where Byron said he'd be. He was an intimidating animal. Owen knew how vicious Bob could be. He'd seen it with his own eyes. An angry, charging bull wasn't something anyone wanted to be in the way of.

Dylan had enlisted each of his men to make an attempt to befriend the bull. He was under the impression that Bob would react to at least one human being with a kindred spirit. So far, Owen was the only one gifted with that privilege, if it could be called that. And it was barely a gift, as sometimes Bob the Bull didn't care if it was Owen or one of the random ranch hands. He was going to act however he wanted to act.

Owen's heart slammed in his chest. He licked his lips, his eyes steady on the beast pacing back and forth in the field. Bob was snorting and kicking the dirt with his feet, which Owen took to be a sign of irritation.

"Anybody figure out what bothered him so much he got out of his pen?"

"I think there was a possum in there in there," one of the other ranch hands called out.

Owen sighed heavily. "Well, did anybody get rid of the possum?"

He looked around at the men, all shaking their heads.

He understood why they hadn't done anything, though. Bob's barn was his and his alone. Owen was one of the few the bull would allow in his private quarters, even to muck it out and clean it. They didn't want to die trying to clean a barn.

He braced himself, wondering what mood Bob would be in this day.

He took a few steps toward the bull and stopped. He always kept his eyes on the animal when he had to approach Bob. When the bull met his gaze, Owen would know what mood he was in.

He took a few more steps. The bull was still

nodding his head, shaking it back and forth, snorting, kicking.

Owen wondered if he should say anything. Should he start walking toward the barn? Or the animal himself?

He decided it would show Bob he could be trusted if he got rid of the possum or whatever critter drove Bob from his home.

With one eye on the animal, he began to walk toward the barn.

"What you doin'?" Byron called out. "Talk to Bob. Get him to calm down."

"I'm going to look for that possum first," Owen replied firmly. "If I get rid of the threat, Bob will know I'm his friend." He glanced at several of the other men making a circle around the cow pasture. "Any one of you could have done this, too."

The light in the barn was dim, but Owen could see enough to do a quick search. Sure enough, not only did Owen find a possum nestled in the hay, he found babies snuggled up to her in safety of the barn.

"Not so safe now, is it?" he whispered, shaking his head. "Come on, family. You gotta move."

Looking around, Owen found an empty sack draped over one of the unoccupied stall doors near him. No one in the possum family seemed disturbed by his presence or the fact that he was trying to move them.

Once they were all in the sack, he took them outside and, in front of the bull, who remained thirty yards away, set the sack on the ground, open. He gently shooed the possum out, and she skittered away, babies on their mother, through the grass and away from the general area.

Owen stood up and looked at Bob. The beast looked back at him. Owen almost felt a kinship with the creature, a feeling that was momentary and fleeting.

Bob the bull stopped pacing and snorting. He turned in the direction of his pen and walked slowly and casually as if he'd never had a problem in the first place. When he reached the break in the outer fence that surrounded his pasture, he stepped over it casually.

"Look at that," Byron came up behind him to say. "Like he ain't even responsible for all that panic. He don't care a smidge."

"I think you might be right," Owen chuckled. "And now I gotta get back to the party. Have I got a story for Sophia."

13

Sophia almost jumped out of her skin when she felt a hand rest on her shoulder. Her head whipped to the side, and she saw it was Owen. Relief swept through her. She hadn't felt panic like that for many years.

He yanked his hand from her, his eyes widening. "I didn't mean to scare you," he said quickly.

She felt like grabbing his hand and putting it back where it had been. "It's okay," she said. "They are bringing out the cake soon. Do you want to go around and play some of the games while we can? I don't think Collin will mind, will you, baby?"

Sophia looked down into the stroller at the sleeping infant. She turned her eyes back up to Owen. "He doesn't seem to mind."

"Let's do it then. I'll bet I can pop more balloons than you on the dart game."

Sophia raised her eyebrows and gave him a haughty look. "Is that so? I suppose we will have to find out, won't we?"

He let himself smile for a moment but then donned a serious expression again. "Yes, I reckon we will."

The day seemed to whizz by. Sophia made sure to keep one eye on the little boys, all three of them, just in case Lucy wasn't watching for a moment while still giving attention to Owen. She was impressed by his dart-throwing skills and told him so.

"I am pretty good at aiming," he replied happily, donning the child-like demeanor Sophia noticed he was fond of. "You should see me shoot a gun."

"There's a competition in a couple of weeks," she informed him. "I would love to see you compete in that. Barney Trampers always wins, and he's not even that good of a shot."

Owen laughed. "If that's the case, how come he's always winning?"

Sophia grinned at him. "That's obvious, you silly man. Everyone around here is terrible."

She felt a great sense of satisfaction when he

burst out with fresh laughter. This time, when he rested his hand on her shoulder, she didn't flinch or pull away. She let the feeling of the weight of his hand fill her with warmth.

The guests of the birthday party seemed to share in Sophia and Owen's good feelings. She was pleased to see so many smiling faces around her. Families had brought all manner of pets, and having the boys with her made the petting zoo the place to be.

She wheeled Collin to a special table that had a chair missing so she could sit and watch as the cake was wheeled out, and Muddy got to shriek with excitement. As spoiled as he might have appeared to others, Sophia noticed with joy there were no unhappy faces in the crowd. Not even the children had a shred of jealousy in their expressions, and that's where Sophia would have expected it.

Owen pulled out a chair at the same table. "Mind if I sit with you?"

Sophia grinned at him, pulling Collin from the stroller to place him on her lap. She turned him so he could face the action and wrapped both arms around his middle so there was no chance he would fall in any direction.

"Look at that," she exclaimed, leaning down slightly and looking around at Collin's face. He had a wide-eyed delighted expression that thrilled her heart. "Isn't that a lovely cake? I'll get you a slice when we're all done singing. You want some cake?" She continued to talk in a sweet voice until Dylan lifted Muddy up on his shoulders so everyone could see the little boy.

"It's time for the birthday song," he announced. He already had everyone's attention because of the cake, so he lifted his son's hands in the air and turned in a careful circle, beginning the song loud and clear in his bold, tenor voice.

Sophia moved Collin's arms in a similar fashion as the song went on. When it was done, she clapped Collin's hands together gently, and the baby giggled and bounced on her lap. She felt a keen sense of affection for the child fill her and couldn't resist giving him a tight hug.

"Such a sweet boy," she gushed, holding him tight as she got to her feet.

"No, please, you sit," Owen stated firmly, standing up at the same time while holding one hand out in her direction. "I'll get some cake for you both. And a refreshing drink, too. For you. I don't think he's drinking real drinks yet, is he?"

Sophia gave him a look. Her attraction to him was increasing by the hour.

She nodded. "That would be so nice of you, Owen. Thank you. I don't want to brave the crowd with Collin. He might get crushed."

Owen chuckled. "Yes, the chaos is amazing. Must be a delicious cake."

Sophia laughed with him and watched as he went to brave the crowd around the table where the cake was being served. At one point, he turned, put his feet together, and put one fist over his heart, giving her a solemn look. Then he saluted as if he was in the army, turned on his heel, and walked the rest of the way valiantly.

By the time he got to the cake table, the crowd had formed something of a line, but one of the girls serving the cake turned and handed him one. Sophia watched him say something to her. He twisted at the waist and pointed back at her. She smiled, lifting one hand to wave.

The girl, who was a temporary day hire from a Bighorn agency, acknowledged her and said something that made Owen lower his head and blush.

Sophia was dying to know what the woman said. She hurried to grab another plate with a full piece of cake on it and placed an empty plate under that one. Handing them both to Owen, she said something, and he returned with something. Sophia would have killed to be a speck of dust on his shoulder at that moment.

She waited with bated breath as he came back to the table.

"I'll have to get the drinks now," he said, placing the cake down. "I didn't think about the fact that I only have two hands."

"What did that girl say to you?"

Owen gave her an innocent look, but she wasn't buying it. She lowered her eyelids. "I know she said something that made you blush, Owen. What did she say? You have to tell me, or I will simply die."

She dramatically placed the back of one hand on her forehead, her eyes closed.

Owen laughed. "She said I have a nice-looking family."

Sophia's eyes widened. She dropped her eyes to Collin before sliding them to the girl who had given them the cake. She was busy with other guests.

"She didn't recognize Collin?" Sophia asked, flabbergasted that anyone could make that mistake in Bighorn. "That girl doesn't know anything about the town she lives in."

She shook her head in disbelief. It wasn't until a few moments later that she realized why Owen had blushed. Her surprise turned to flirtation when she set her gaze on the man.

"I think you will be a wonderful father to your children someday," she said.

Owen pressed his lips together, his eyes twinkling with delight. He lifted one finger in the air, pointing up. "One moment," he said. "Let me get a drink for us. I'm parched."

Sophia watched as he lit off again, this time in search of the drinks table, which he found two down from the one he'd previously been at.

Sophia fed bits of the cake to Collin while she waited for Owen to return. He loved the fluffiness of the cake and the sweetness of the icing. Sophia managed to feed him the lower half of her slice before Owen got back.

"Whoa," Owen said appreciatively. "He likes cake."

"He sure does. He can have all of mine if he wants. I don't particularly like it."

"You are a kind woman, Sophia."

He slid into his seat and grinned at her as he dug into his food and drank his cold tea.

14

The sun was dropping in the sky, but there were several hours of daylight before dusk. Still, Sophia could tell her tiny charges, and even the little ones' parents were looking a bit worse for wear. She reached out to brush the hair from Felix's eyes when he balled up his fists and pressed them into his closed eyelids.

"You look tired, darling," Sophia said in a soft voice. "Let me take you to the nursery. I think it's time you had a short nap."

Sophia knew that keeping the children up until late in the afternoon and then giving them a nap might likely have them up at the wee hours of the morning. But it was cruel to keep Felix awake, especially when Collin was allowed to sleep whenever he wanted.

She didn't see Muddy, but the birthday boy was in Lucy's care. It was best to leave his naptime—if he got one—to her. She'd be the one to know just how worn out the child was.

Owen had stayed with her the entire time, often having long conversations with other guests, but he was always within earshot of her. She wondered if he did that on purpose or if it was just a coincidence.

She had a feeling it was the former. Should she tell him she was taking the boys to their nursery? Was it his business?

Sophia was still determined not to let Owen think he was obligated to her just because he'd taken her out for one meal. She decided he was busy and would see her when she came back. He was seated at the table they'd occupied the whole day and was now talking to Byron.

"Tired, Sophieee, tired." Sophia liked the way the little boy pronounced her name. She grinned and tapped him lightly on the bottom of his chin before taking his hand. He looked up at her with the biggest blue eyes, and she felt a wash of affection flow through her.

She leaned down and scooped him up, so he was essentially sitting on her forearm. Pushing the stroller ahead of her, she had to stop when she reached the stairs, as the only way to get the stroller up was to jog it and lift its wheels or just pick the whole thing up.

Instead, she reached in and lifted the baby out.

With a little boy on each hip, Sophia strolled through the glass double doors from the back porch, grateful that one of them was propped open with a large stone. The inside of the house was nearly as active as the outside, if not more, now that the day was winding down.

She nodded and smiled at a few of the guests who saw her and whispered behind their hands with non-malicious looks in their eyes. Sophia felt warm inside as she went up the stairs to take the boys to the nursery.

It was much quieter on the second floor. Although she could still hear the hum of voices downstairs and the distant strains of the musicians in the backyard, Sophia enjoyed the silence around her as she got the boys ready for their beds.

"In the morning, we will have fun," she sang a little tune as she worked in a gentle, soft voice. "We will dance and sing all day long. And when the day is through, we'll put on our pajamas and say good night to yoooouu." She was making it up as she went along, but Felix didn't seem to mind. Collin, for his part, kept his big blue eyes on her, too, as she sang. She wondered if he was thinking she was a crazy woman for singing off-key.

"I'm not singing off-key." She put her face close to the baby's and fluttered her eyelashes at him, making him giggle. "I'm singing in perfect harmony." She giggled and kissed Collin's fat cheek. "That doesn't even make sense, does it?" she asked him. She waited a moment as if he was answering her. She grabbed him around his belly and tickled him. "Why am I asking you? Huh? That makes even less sense."

Felix was crawling into his bed, his pajama top not buttoned, his eyes half-closed.

Sophia hurried to finish off the buttons and tucked him in. "You sleep tight, my darling boy," she said, kissing him on the nose, "and when you wake up, you will have lots of more fun things to do. Okay?"

Felix grinned. She couldn't get over how precious he was, how much he looked like his mother. Muddy took after his father's looks while Collin and Felix both resembled their mother. Sophia had a feeling their youngest baby would end up a perfect mix between the two parents.

She would have sworn she heard Felix beginning to snore when she turned away but didn't see how it could be possible for someone to fall asleep in zero seconds. Even at two and a half years old.

Collin was sitting in his crib when Sophia turned back to him. He leaned forward, his eyes locked on her in an almost uncomfortable way. She watched in amazement when the boy pulled himself toward the railing on the side of his crib and proceeded to stand up.

Sophia had never seen him stand up on his own. His little legs wobbled, but he was standing.

"Oh, Collin," she cried out a bit breathlessly. She couldn't be as jubilant as she wanted to be because it would surely wake Felix if she yelled and cheered and did somersaults.

Instead, she crossed the room in a few steps, swept him out of the crib, and held him up in the air above her head, spinning and dancing with him. He giggled delightedly, clapping his tiny hands together.

"You are a genius," she exaggerated for his benefit. "You are brilliant. You will be a man among men.

A man to be respected. A man with dignity, style, and class."

Collin stared at her as if she'd lost her mind. She did one last spin before placing him back in the crib. He immediately dropped to his bottom.

"Well, we can't have everything, can we?" Sophia said with a laugh. She reached into the crib and tousled his hair. "Good job, little man. I'm so proud of you. And I can't wait to tell your momma and papa. They are going to go a little bit crazy, you know?" She held her thumb and index finger a half-inch from each other. "Just a little bit."

Sophia was glad when the child dropped back and turned over on his side, closing his eyes. She covered him with a light blanket so he wouldn't get too warm.

After she settled him in, she went around the crib to look through the window there. She could see the backyard. She focused on Owen and Byron, imagining what they were talking about. Were they talking about her? Was it her they were searching for when they did a sweep of the guests still remaining at the party? She hoped so. She hoped Owen's brain was filled with as much affection for her as she felt for him.

She could see him down there. Neither he nor

Byron had moved from where they were. She moved her eyes from him and searched the grounds for Lucy and Muddy. The boy had to be exhausted by now.

Just as she was about to leave the room, the door opened. Lucy was standing on the other side, looking panicked. Sophia hardly had to ask why she looked that way but did anyway.

"What's wrong? Where's Muddy?"

Lucy seemed to be choking. She put one hand on her throat and held the other one out to Sophia. "Sophia..." she said, barely getting the words out. "I only... I only turned away for a minute. Just a minute, that's all. There were so many other people around. I thought someone would see him if he wandered away. But... oh, Sophia, I can't find him. I can't find him."

Lucy collapsed into Sophia's arms, but Sophia had no time for that. She lowered Lucy to the ground and stepped over the weeping woman. "Get yourself together, Lucy," she breathed. "This is not the time for hysterics. We have to go find him. Everyone will help us look. Come now. You have to come."

"But Mattie and Dylan will be so angry with me," Lucy cried.

Sophia frowned, sudden anger spilling through her. She grabbed Lucy by the arm and pulled her up to her feet.

"Come on. We have to find him. That's more important right now. You have to help. Come on."

15

———

"We don't want to alarm everyone yet," Sophia said, pulling Lucy from the room and closing the door quietly behind her. "We don't want those boys in there worried about their brother either. Well, little Felix and he was asleep. Mattie and Dylan have retired to their room, I think, but they are changing into their dinner clothes. They'll be going out tonight." Sophia's panicked heart quaked in her chest. "Unless we don't find Muddy. You check in the other rooms up here. I'll check his room. We'll search the house before we go out there."

"What if someone took him?" Lucy asked breathlessly.

Sophia's chest tightened to an anguishing point.

"No, that's not what happened. He wandered off. We'll find him. Don't think like that. Look around up here and meet me in the foyer. We'll search everywhere we can before we alert anyone else."

"But the more people looking for him the better, isn't that so?"

Sophia felt properly chastised, even though Lucy had done no such thing.

"You're right. But not everyone. Not yet. Let's tell the staff to look for him. And the ranch hands can look around outside. If we don't find him, we'll need more people to search further. I just don't want everyone to panic until we've checked to make sure he isn't simply hiding under one of the tables."

Lucy gave her a skeptical look that Sophia knew was justified. Muddy was a little boy on fire and loved the attention he'd gotten for his birthday. But that didn't mean he didn't get tired and fall asleep hidden away from everyone.

"Let's find him, Lucy. We've got to."

They nodded at each other, and as she hurried down the hallway, Lucy said over her shoulder, "I'll get Dennis. He needs to know to look, too."

Sophia only nodded to acknowledge she'd heard, grabbed her skirt in one hand, and ran down the stairs sliding her other hand along the railing, so she had balance. Her heart was beating a mile a minute. Every muscle in her body was tense.

"Oh, Muddy," she murmured as she flew through the double doors to the backyard. There were still two dozen guests walking around. Most of the animals in the petting zoo had gone home with their owners. The only children Sophia could see were in the arms of their parents, tired out.

She made her way around the backyard, quietly lifting table skirts to look under and see if the child was hiding.

Muddy was nowhere to be found. Sophia was fighting back tears by the time she got to where the ranch hands were seated, all around several tables where the guests had previously been sitting. Owen saw her coming. She could tell he was happy to see her approaching at first, but then his face changed. He could tell she was upset. Concern filled his features, and he shot to his feet.

"Sophia," he said, keeping his voice low as if he already knew her problem might cause a panic. "What's wrong?"

Sophia dropped her head down and lowered her eyes, not able to look directly at him. The guilt she was feeling was getting heavier as time went on. "It's Muddy," she hissed. "We can't find him. I don't know what could possibly have happened to him. Lucy is looking through the house to see if he's playing hide and seek. But I've looked all around out here, and I don't see him. If he's hiding, he's hiding well."

"I haven't heard anyone calling for him. Who else is looking?"

"I wanted to have an initial look around before saying anything," Sophia replied, now unsure of her decision. "I didn't want to start a panic. But I think it's time to let everyone know so everyone will look. Mattie and Dylan have both gone inside to change clothes and rest. I will have to tell them."

"You do that. We'll start looking." He turned away from her and barked orders at the men behind him, who all jumped to their feet. He wasn't the boss, but in this situation, he was taking charge. Sophia was distracted for a moment by her admiration.

It only lasted a moment, and she snapped out of it, spinning around to rush back to the house. Lucy was just coming to the double glass doors when she went through them. Sophia had no hope that the maid had found Muddy. Her face and the fact that the boy wasn't with her said it all.

"The men are starting a search," Sophia said.

"I'm going to go tell Dylan and Mattie. Go out and tell the guests what's happened."

"Sophia. Sophia!"

She twisted around sharply to see Owen running toward the house. He was followed by a tall man and a short woman. The man was holding a little boy who looked terrified.

She hurried back out to meet them at the top of the stairs, her eyes shifting from one to the other worriedly.

"What is it?" she asked frantically.

When Owen spoke, he did so quickly. "This is Corey. His little piglet is missing. We think Muddy must have run after it when it got out of the petting zoo."

"Oh no." Sophia covered her mouth with one hand, her wide eyes turning to the little boy, who looked about five. He had his arms wrapped around his father's neck and was pressing his face into the man's shoulder.

"I'm sorry," he was crying softly, "I'm sorry."

"It's all right, Corey," Sophia said quickly, hurrying to place one hand on the boy's back comfortingly. "It's all right. We're going to find your little piglet and Muddy, too. What's your piglet's name?"

"Barney."

"Barney the pig." Sophia gave him an appreciative smile. "I like it. Well, we're going to find him, okay? And we'll bring him back to you as quick as we can. Thank you for telling us." She looked at the man holding Corey. "We'll bring the piglet to you when we find it," she said. "I assume Mattie or Dylan know where you live?"

"They do," the man replied with a nod. "I'm sorry. I didn't know this happened. We would have stopped it if we—"

"No need to apologize. A lot of errors were made by us adults today. Go ahead on home, and we'll let you know as soon as we know something."

"Thank you."

The family turned away, the man and woman sharing a worried look.

Sophia didn't want to waste any more time. "Give me five minutes to let Dylan and Mattie know what's going on before you start yelling out for Muddy. They probably went into the woods since that's where animals and children love to explore. I know Muddy enjoys our trips and hikes into the forest."

Sophia hoped she was giving the impression of someone confident in what they were doing and saying. Her fear that something dreadful had happened to Muddy was almost overwhelming. She had to rein it in and keep it under control, or she wouldn't be able to think straight. It was bad enough that she had to tell Mattie and Dylan their son was missing. The birthday boy. The light of his father's eye.

"I should be the one to tell Mattie and Dylan," Lucy said quickly. "I was the one who was supposed to be watching him. I only turned away for a moment. That's all. I didn't notice he wasn't with the other children when they were playing in the zoo."

"How long ago did you notice Barney was missing?" Sophia asked Corey, hoping he could understand the question. She could tell by the way he blinked and his blank expression that he didn't.

His father shook his head. "We asked him the same thing. He doesn't know. He can't tell us."

Sophia nodded, turning her eyes away, thinking hard. "All right. I think we can safely assume the piglet and Muddy went straight from the petting zoo to the woods. Let's spread out from that point and go toward the trees. Wait to start yelling out for about five minutes but start heading that way now. Time is of the essence now."

16

Sophia tried valiantly to hold in her tears as she rushed through the house to Mattie and Dylan's master bedroom. She paused only for a second, her hand up to knock. She was nervous even though she hadn't been in charge of Muddy. She was the nanny, and it stood to reason that even if Lucy was the one looking after Muddy at the time, he was her charge, and she should have been checking on him.

She knocked three times and turned the knob when she heard, "Come in."

The master bedroom was gigantic. It took several hours to get it clean. Mattie was seated at her dressing table, patting her hair, while Dylan was leaning back against the doorjamb to the washroom which was attached. He had one hand deep in his pocket and holding a smoking pipe to his lips.

Mattie looked at Sophia in the mirror, and Dylan gave her a smile when she entered.

Both expressions immediately changed when they saw her for more than a second.

Mattie turned swiftly in her seat and gripped the back of the chair. "Sophia? What's happened?"

Dylan pushed off the doorjamb, his face turning sober.

"It's Muddy," Sophia said quietly, trying not to show how terrified she was. "He's run off. Probably into the woods after a stray piglet that got out of the petting zoo."

"What?" Dylan asked sternly. Sophia knew he'd heard what she said and was questioning whether he'd heard it right or not.

"I'm sorry. I was in the nursery putting the two younger boys down for a nap, and Lucy came in to say she couldn't find him. Then a couple brought over their son, and the little boy said his piglet had run off. He couldn't tell me when or if he'd seen Muddy run after the animal. Everyone is—" She stopped abruptly when the first cries of "Peter, and Muddy, and Barney," could be heard outside.

Mattie's eyes widened as she jumped to her feet.

In the next moment, she was in front of her husband, both hands on his chest, her pleading eyes gazing up at him. "Dylan, We have to find Muddy. We have to find him, Dylan."

"We will," Dylan replied, reaching up to wrap his fingers around her wrists. He leaned in to give her a quick kiss. "We'll find him. Come on. You, too, Sophia. Let's go find my son."

He stomped out the door, practically dragging Mattie along with him, as she seemed to be having a hard time staying on her feet.

Sophia followed quickly behind him, her heart aching and wrenching every time she heard the voices outside calling out the name of the little boy and the piglet.

Dylan looked over his shoulder at her. "Barney is the name of the piglet, I assume?"

Sophia nodded.

He did the same. In the next moment, the three of them were outside, racing across the short green grass to where the ranch hands, the house staff, and the remaining guests were spreading out over the lawn, calling out for the missing boy and pet.

Sophia looked for Owen. The only way she would be able to do this with the strength she needed was if she was near him. She'd never relied on the presence of a man to give her strength before, she thought. But she couldn't help it. She'd fallen for his charms at their dinner together, and it was hard to think about independence now that she'd given her heart away.

Owen was with Byron and several other men near one of the barns, the one closest to the forest. He was holding a large map between his hands, spread out so that the others standing behind him, looking over his shoulders, could see what he was seeing.

Sophia took a moment to think about how brilliant Owen was before running to the men to see if she could help.

When she was close enough, Owen glanced up at her.

"Sophia," he said in a curt way, "this map is crude, but it should at least let us know where there are deep holes from old wells and other objects that Muddy might hide behind or get hurt by."

Fear pierced Sophia's heart. She had only been thinking about Muddy being lost. She hadn't thought about the many dangers the forest represented for a five-year-old and a piglet he was probably caring more about than himself.

"Oh no," she breathed.

Owen gave her a sharp look. "Keep yourself together, my dear. We're going to need your strength and your bond with him when we find him."

Sophia took his words to heart, pulled in a deep breath, and squared her shoulders. "All right," she said, nodding curtly. "Show me the map, and I will let anyone else know what to expect."

Sophia looked over the map and memorized it the best she could while Owen talked to the other men about how they would go about doing the search.

"How far could he really have gotten on those short legs of his?" one of the ranch hands, a younger man just out of his teens, had a note of affection and fear in his voice when he spoke.

"Far enough to get lost," another ranch hand responded. He was a taller, older man who gave the younger one a look a father might give his son in a crisis situation such as this. The younger man nodded, his eyes returning to Owen.

"Sophia, you need to stay with Mattie because when we bring him back, you two are the ones he will want. I'm thinking Dylan is going to go on the search with us. The guests should stay out of the forest unless they've hunted this land before and know it well."

"You should be telling this to Dylan and Mattie," Sophia mentioned.

Owen shook his head. "Well, I'm telling it to you. You go tell them. Don't forget about the obstacles in the woods, and make sure to mention them if anyone seems determined to give it a hike anyway."

Sophia moved her eyes over the group of men surrounding Owen, who were murmuring instructions and comments to each other, a few of them pointing out parts on the map they knew well.

"I'll get to that right now." Sophia turned to go back to where Mattie and Dylan were discussing matters with the house staff near the table that had adorned a delightfully decorated birthday cake just hours before.

Owen grabbed her arm before she could take off and made her turn back to him. The other ranch hands must have sensed something because Sophia was astounded to see every single one of them turn away at the very same time. Byron even slipped the map out of Owen's hand, and Owen didn't seem to notice.

"Sophia."

His voice was so filled with emotion, Sophia's heart melted in her chest. She swallowed, unable to get out a proper response. She was ashamed to make some kind of guttural noise in her throat that came out like a grunted question. She raised her eyebrows, hoping she wasn't blushing too furiously.

"I don't want you thinking this is your fault. I know you probably feel like it is, but it isn't. I want you to know that no matter what happens, no matter what, this is not your fault. If anything, it's the darn piglet's fault for being cute and breaking out of the petting zoo fence."

Sophia swallowed again, this time to keep down the tears that threatened to fall.

She nodded but couldn't say anything. He put one hand on her arm and squeezed. It was as if he'd shocked her with lightning. Her entire body tingled. Their eyes were locked until they both heard Byron say Owen's name. The connection between them dissolved, and they turned away from each other at the same time.

17

When the men knew where they were going, and the search team was set in place, Owen ran his eyes around the lawn for Sophia. She was still with Mattie and Dylan. Mattie was distraught, and Owen understood why. Dylan looked angry. Owen could tell by the way the boss was avoiding looking at Lucy, even when the maid was speaking, that he blamed the girl for what had happened.

Owen prayed Muddy would be found safe, or Lucy would likely feel the full extent of Dylan's wrath. And Mattie's pain.

They started at the broken fence. Byron led the way, watching the ground as if he could see the little footsteps Muddy and the piglet had left behind.

Once they got to the forest, they started calling his name repeatedly and loudly.

"Muddy," Owen yelled, sweeping his eyes over the myriad of trees that surrounded him. His chest hurt with worry. Why had the boy taken such a risk? Even at five, he should have known better than to go running off into the forest. Owen had to clear his throat of the panicked tears that choked him. "Muddy! Where are you, son? You aren't in trouble. Everybody is worried about you. Please come out if you're hiding. Muddy. Muddy!"

Owen sucked in a deep breath and took a few more steps into the woods. He could see Byron to his left and Luke, another ranch hand, to his right. Byron was staring at the ground with a perplexed look on his face. He lifted his eyes to see Owen looking at him and shook his head. Owen took that to mean he couldn't see any kind of tracks to follow.

He nodded at his friend, trying to give him a sympathetic look but probably not succeeding. All he could feel at that moment was fear. Fear that the boy wouldn't be alive when he was found.

It had only been a few hours at the very most. The problem, in Owen's mind, was that there were dangers in the woods that Muddy would have no way to escape. Snakes and bears and mountain lions and well holes that hadn't been properly covered up... that was only the tip of the iceberg. He could be hurt in so many ways.

"Muddy!" Owen traipsed through the woods, hearing the calls of his friends and neighbors around him. Why wouldn't he come out? Where could he possibly be? "Muddy. You aren't in trouble."

Owen felt like if he was a five-year-old, he probably would hide until dark and then sneak back home. That way, he wouldn't be on full display when he returned, subject to the scrutiny of everyone who searched for him. He hoped that wasn't the way Muddy was, but if he was alive, he certainly wasn't showing himself.

"Muddy, please show yourself," Byron called out. "Muddy, come on, buddy, let us know where you are. Momma is worried, and Papa is worried. Everybody's worried. Come on, Muddy."

When there was still no response, Byron came over to where Owen was searching.

"This is real bad, Owen. We're pretty far into the woods now, and nobody has seen hide or hair of the kid. Where could he be? Do you think he's in one of the well holes? We should check them all. You got that map?"

Owen thought it was a good idea to start with the

wells. He pulled the rolled-up map out of his back pocket and stretched it open in front of him. "There." He nodded at one because he was using both hands. He tapped Byron's hand with his so the other man would take that side of the map. He pointed after Byron took it.

"I'll check these two. You check those two. We'll meet here by the big oak where the trail forks. You see that?"

"I see it."

"Okay. When we meet back up, we'll pick more holes to check and some of the other places where there could be a problem."

Byron nodded and took another glance at the map, his eyes darting from the paper to the trees around him as he got his bearings. He dropped the corner of the map and took off in the direction of the holes he was to look for.

For a moment, Owen wondered if he should give the map to Byron. But his friend had been employed on the Sullivan land longer and knew it better. Owen just happened to be the one who came upon the map of the land. It had been left in the bunkhouse by a previous ranch hand who had a knack for map drawing. He left the Sullivan employment to pursue a career in that very industry.

He wished there was more than one. There was no time to create a new map based on the old one, but Owen made a mental note to get that done before he was done with his employment there.

The grass in the forest had grown but was kept down by the deer and other animals that fed on it, plus the trees above blocked a great deal of sunlight.

It wasn't long before Owen came up on the first hole from a well dug many years ago. It had been grown over, so it was not noticeable probably in the first years after it was abandoned. He only saw it because he was looking for it.

Nevertheless, it had a solid round cover that Owen had to push hard to move. There was little chance the boy had slipped into the depths of that well unless he was put there on purpose.

The new line of thinking sent a chill through Owen. He couldn't imagine anyone kidnapping Muddy and taking the child's life, throwing him down a well afterward. Owen said intense prayers as he pushed hard on the round stone covering the large hole.

He didn't want to even look. But he reminded himself that the chances of someone taking Muddy on purpose at his own birthday party were slim. He looked down into the depths but couldn't see the bottom. He would have to satisfy himself that the child wasn't there. If he was never found, this would be the last place they would check. Just to make sure.

Owen wasn't about to leave the stone cover off the hole even a little bit. He went to the other side and pushed the cover back over the old well.

Owen tried to other two holes from the map, and neither of them had a child stuck in them. He went to the spot where he was to meet Byron to find that his friend was already there. As soon as he was within hearing distance, Byron said in a loud voice. "I didn't find Muddy. Not even a sign of him. You?"

"No. No sign of him. There are only a few more holes, but there are some downed trees, and of course we have to check the stream. I'm gonna scream if that boy is down in the watering hole staring into the rippling water. Kids get fascinated by stuff like that, you know."

Byron nodded. "Yeah, it would be aggravating, but it would be a big relief, too."

Owen had to agree with that. "More than a big relief. Let's check out these places together. We can cover a lot of ground, too."

"I've been keeping my eye out but haven't seen a thing. I can't believe he even got this far."

"If he went near the water, he might have crossed over the bridge."

"I think it all depends on where that daggone piglet went," Owen grumbled. "And that could have gone anywhere. It wouldn't lead him to the water, but it would go over the bridge. Pigs are smart critters."

"They sure are. And you're right. Lemme get Luke and Dexter. We'll all go to the other side of the bridge and start checking over there. Get some of the others to go up and down the river, calling out and looking for him."

"I'm just praying he's found alive," Owen mumbled. "I don't want to be around Dylan and Mattie when they find out. I don't wanna be the one to tell them, either."

"Know what you mean," Byron replied, plunging one hand through his blond hair. "I wouldn't either."

The two men hurried to the next spot where a hole had been dug. It was obvious to Owen the initial construction of the well was abandoned after about five feet was dug out of the ground.

"Wonder what this was all about?" he asked, studying the crevasse. "They never finished it."

"Must've had other plans. He could have crawled out of that on his own. Glad he isn't here."

"Me, too. The next one is over there."

Owen and Byron checked the last two holes and checked the parts on the map that looked questionable. They were at the bridge, staring over to the other side, watching for a little boy to emerge from the forest.

"Muddy," Byron shouted, nearly making Owen come out of his skin. "Where are you, boy?"

18

———

Sophia couldn't stand to wait at the house. Mattie, Dylan, Lucy, and the others were scouring the land closest to the house, including the inside in their search. They called out for the boy over and over to no avail.

Sophia didn't think Muddy would be found at the house. If he was anywhere, and if he was safe, it was somewhere in the woods. She looked over her shoulder at the men as they disappeared into the trees of the forest.

She wanted to be with them. She didn't want to stay where she was doing no good.

A thought entered her mind. When Muddy was found, he would be terrified and probably hungry as a result. Most children seemed to be hungry when they were frightened. She was under that impression anyway.

Instead of going around the house to look for the boy as she'd been instructed by Dylan, Sophia went back into the house through a different side door that was practically unnoticeable from most places in the backyard. It was a servant's entrance, but the house staff was allowed to use any entrance they wanted since they were not enslaved.

The door led directly into the kitchen. A huge pantry was to her left, behind a door labeled *Foodstuffs*.

Sophia went into the pantry and looked around. There were sacks of flour and sugar on the floor, along with other ingredients, and shelves lined the walls on three sides. She went to the fruits and grabbed a bowl filled with oranges. Pigs like oranges, she believed. And so do little boys. She grabbed three of them and shoved them into the pockets of her apron. As she left the pantry, she noticed the oranges banged against her legs painfully. She couldn't go through the woods trying to find a child with oranges beating her legs to death. She'd be covered in bruises.

Thinking more carefully, Sophia decided oranges weren't all she needed. What if he was hurt?

She might need bandages. She might need to clean him up, which would require a towel. But how could she carry all these things? She couldn't fit it all in the pockets of her apron, that was for sure.

Sophia swept her eyes around the room, looking for a solution. In the corner, she saw a sack lying flat on the floor. She hurried over to it and was a little disappointed to see it had carried onions in its previous employment. The last one in the sack rolled out and tapped against the tip of her toes.

She bent over and looked at it, pondering whether to take it or not.

But, since the bag itself stunk highly of onions, she decided not to add to it by bringing along a healthy ripe one.

She set the onion on a shelf nearby so it would be used when it was needed. Carrying the sack back out, she used the strap to hold it on, crossing it over one shoulder and draping it against the opposite hip. She put the oranges in it and added two apples, a bunch of broccoli, and two celery sticks. She left the pantry behind and went straight across to the sink, which had a shelf above it. On the shelf, she saw the two canteens she'd seen sitting there practically since the day she was hired.

Confident no one used them, she pumped water

into them and sealed them tight. Into her sack they went, and she was back out the door onto the lawn, trying to look nonchalant. She spotted Mattie and Dylan, who had come back together in a hug by the fence of the petting zoo. Mattie was crying. Dylan was holding her. Sophia knew it had to be very hard for Dylan to be strong when he was terrified just as much as everyone else.

She slipped past those who were near her, catching snippets of conversations that were all about the missing child and how devastated the Sullivans would be if he wasn't found safe and sound. And alive.

Sophia's heart ached. She prayed hard that she would find the boy and bring him back to his parents. If not her, the men were looking hard, searching through the woods just beyond the petting zoo. How far could the child have gone? Wouldn't he respond to their calls if he could?

Sophia refused to let herself cry. That would be a sign that she was giving in and not plunging ahead like she always did. It had been a long time since she'd had to make quick decisions to save someone's life, if not her own.

Once Sophia was in the woods, the first thing she did was head for the river. She might come across one of the ranch hands, but she wouldn't be in trouble with them. Maybe they would be able to tell her if there was any news, any clues at all. Byron was a good tracker. He might pick up one single footprint out of the entire forest that could lead them to Muddy and Barney.

She racked her brain, trying to think of places Muddy had gone before. She didn't know why he would do that, though, when he wasn't in trouble and had just chased a pig into the woods. Wouldn't he grab the piglet and come back to the party?

He would, she surmised, if he could.

Something *had* to be wrong. There was just no way around that.

Sophia immediately choked on a sudden rush of tears, lifting one hand to her cover her mouth, squinting her eyes, and jerking her shoulders forward. She wasn't going to weep like a baby. *She wasn't giving up.*

She shook her head vigorously and wiped her eyes.

Clutching the sack like a security blanket, Sophia trotted ahead, ignoring the biting sting of thorns that grabbed at her ankles and brushed against her knees, catching in the hem of her dress. She had to pull hard to get it off one particular stubborn twig jutting from a haphazard-looking bush.

Sophia stopped, picturing herself as Muddy, short, stubby legs moving through this thick brush. It was unlikely. Plus, there was no trail from even a small animal, and Barney would have left *something*.

She turned away from the bushes she was facing and swept her eyes over her surroundings, looking for a better trail. She spotted one through the brush and was amazed she had stopped in just the right place to even see it. She leaned forward just an inch, and it disappeared. It was the same when she leaned back slightly.

Feeling grateful, Sophia turned and headed for the opening. The trail she'd seen was in a very open spot, a field with heavily overgrown grass and plenty of weeds but no trees and bushes that were difficult to get through.

A child would be more likely to come through an area like this, as would a small animal like Barney.

Sophia found what looked like a recent trail where the tall grass had been trodden upon so much it had bent over almost in allegiance. Relief filled her. She sighed and continued down that trail instead.

Before she knew it, she was nearing the bridge.

She could see it in the distance, jutting up and over the river, which was about a hundred yards at its smallest width. The bridge had been built over that area.

Sophia could hear water bubbling. She felt moisture in the air. One part of the river had to be near. It seemed she was destined to be the one to look in the water for the child she had grown to love.

Sophia emerged from the trees onto the thirty-yard beach area, where the sand below her feet was the same as it was by the Atlantic Ocean.

The bridge was completely clear now from one side to the other.

But it wasn't the bridge Sophia's eyes went to.

It was what was in the sky beyond the bridge.

She sucked in a sharp breath as she took in the dark clouds invading the blue that had given them such a nice day.

"No," she murmured, terrified. "Not now."

19

Owen felt water in the air. He could tell they were getting close to Bonsack River. No one had reported even a sign of the child. He was beginning to feel not just helpless but confused, as well. Muddy couldn't have simply disappeared. The woods were vast, that was true. There were plenty of places to hide that would prevent the men from finding Muddy. That was also true.

But why would Muddy hide? They'd checked the ravines, the holes, the crevices in the ground, all the areas where there was a sudden drop. No sign of a healthy or injured or dead child.

Owen shivered. How could this be happening?

He fought with himself when he tried to lay

blame. How could he when he had never been a nanny and never knew what the job entailed other than keeping an eye on the charges? And Lucy had been in charge of Muddy. From what Owen gathered, Sophia had taken the other two boys into the house. That meant Lucy only had one job.

To make sure Muddy was safe.

An image of the young woman flashed through Owen's mind. Her remorse was real. She claimed she'd only turned away for a moment and that she'd been laughing at the antics of a pet goat playing with a tortoise. The tortoise would move just slightly, and the goat would react as though he was about to have his head chopped off. But he kept coming back and touching his nose to the tortoiseshell, which would make the animal slide his head out of the shell and nip lightly on the goat's nose.

Owen remembered every detail of what Lucy had said as she pleaded to be forgiven.

It wasn't his place to forgive her. He just hoped they found Muddy and everything would be all right with everyone. He wondered if Lucy would still be working at the ranch in the morning.

Leaving his frivolous thoughts behind, Owen concentrated on the river and the bridge ahead. Animals were attracted to water. He was leaning toward a rescue rather than a retrieval. Muddy hadn't been gone for days or weeks. It had been mere hours. He was confident there were no injuries to speak of but knew that was only his ego talking to prevent him from scaring himself and others.

Owen didn't realize he'd been so concentrated on the river that he'd left his reality and went off on a thinking session of his own. He was picturing the bridge in his head, guessing at its structure and how firm it was. There was no real reason to know those answers. It was simply that he had to keep his mind working. When his name was said in an almost panicky voice, he spun around to see it was Luke, who had come along on the same trail as them, going off to scout but always coming back faithfully.

"What is it?" he asked Byron.

Without saying anything, Byron simply pointed.

Owen looked to his left. Mostly, he could only see trees. "What is it, Byron? Just tell me, for God's sake, tell me."

Byron reached out and grabbed Owen's arm, pulling him over to where he was. He was slightly taller than Byron, but he accommodated by bending a little at the waist. Byron had a telescope.

He put the telescope in Owen's hand.

Not one to be ungrateful, he thanked Byron and

put the telescope to his eye. He could see through the trees at the sky beyond.

What he saw horrified him. He stumbled back a step and felt the pressure of Byron's hand on his back. "I don't believe it," he hissed. "I don't believe it. Now. Why didn't it come three hours ago? I don't believe it."

He shoved the telescope back into his friend's hand with a quick "thank you."

With that, he tore through the woods toward the bridge, screaming out Muddy's name. He heard Byron doing the same, except he was crashing through the brush, and Owen could hear him yelling to some of the other men, including Luke, who was the closest to the two of them.

Owen's heart pounded and ached and pounded some more. He found himself short of breath and had to stop for a moment to calm down. It felt as if a child of his own had passed.

He leaned forward, placing his hands on his locked knees, locking his elbows at the same time. He let his head hang for a moment and tried to catch his breath. The storm was coming. They had to find Muddy and get back home as fast as they could. He had no doubt Dylan was taking care of things back at the ranch, having whoever stayed behind batten down the hatches.

But the men, including himself, had come into the woods unprepared for a storm. They'd simply run in through the trees, searching through the brush for the little lost boy and piglet. Most of them weren't wearing their gun belts.

Owen had his, just the one on the right side, and he'd never expected to use it. He ran across the shoreline to the bridge and crossed over it. Moments later, he could hear the beat of the ranch hands' boots coming over behind him.

"Muddy, it's no time to play, son. Time to go home. Bad weather coming. Come out, come out, wherever you are."

Owen tried hard to keep the panic out of his voice. The last thing he wanted to do was scare the child even more than he probably already was.

"Muddy," Byron yelled the boy's name.

"Peter," another ranch hand used the boy's Christian name. "Hey, Peter. You there? Petey!"

Still no answer.

The wind was picking up. Owen felt it on his face. He was going against the wind. The rolling clouds in the distance had only come a little closer. He surmised it was a slow-moving storm. That was somewhat of a relief but possibly and most probably meant only an extension of perhaps an hour at most.

All he wanted to do at that moment was know where the child was off to and go to rescue him. He was still praying the boy would be returned to his mother. Mattie wouldn't live without her son. Not happily anyway. Owen shuddered to think of what she might become if she lost her first-born son.

Owen stayed close to the bridge, turning to the right and searching for footprints on the beach sand. All he saw was sand, sand, and more sand. He knew that if Muddy came down this way, that's all he'd see, too. And it would be so scary. He wouldn't know which direction to turn. He'd be confused, scared, wanting to protect the piglet from harm.

Where would a little boy like that go?

The mountain was close, but not that close. He couldn't see Muddy getting that far. If he crossed the bridge, he would find a place to hide.

"Muddy," he began a new chorus of the child's name being called out to his left and his right as people fanned out in search of the boy. "Muddy, where are you?" "Come out, come out wherever you are."

Owen slowed down when he got nearer to the woods. He wanted to do a careful search, not that his previous searches hadn't been careful. He was reassured that so many had crossed the bridge while there were still people checking the forest on the other side of the river, where they'd just come from.

It might need to be searched several times before they find the child.

He didn't care how many times they had to search. If no one found Muddy, he would work for the Sullivans for the rest of his life just to wait and find out what happened. He'd be searching for the kid in every crowd, through all the trees, and would probably search and search until the whole thing was explained.

He was about to take his first step into the woods when he heard someone cry out. His head darted in that direction, and he spun on his heel, nearly losing his balance. He grabbed a nearby tree to steady himself and then took off over the shoreline sand toward the noise. Other men were running that way. He could see and hear them as he ran.

20

———

Sophia couldn't tell if the clouds were coming toward them or drifting off in another direction. She could only hope they would get out of the way. She ran toward the bridge, listening to the men on the other side calling out for Muddy. She was glad they had gone over. That meant she wouldn't be alone out there looking.

She thought she could hear Owen's voice, and when she got to the bridge, she looked for him.

By the time she got across to the other side, she couldn't hear anyone calling Muddy's name anymore. It was as if the entire search party had disappeared just like the child and the pig.

Helplessness overwhelmed Sophia. She was a

strong woman. She told herself as often as she felt she needed it. It didn't seem to help this time. She felt alone, even though she knew she wasn't.

The next moment, she was telling herself that was exactly how Muddy must be feeling.

But if he was and was hiding away, why wasn't he just coming out and letting them take him home? Was he that ashamed of running after Barney? Her heart ached for the little boy.

A thought struck Sophia like the lightning of the upcoming storm. She blinked rapidly, her mind moving quickly through a lesson she had recently taught Muddy. She'd told him about caves. There were caves around the Sullivan land. She remembered telling Muddy in a nonchalant way. He didn't seem interested until Lucy, who was holding Collin, spoke up, obviously incredibly interested in caves.

Sophia hadn't noticed at the time. But now, looking back, she could see the excitement growing in Muddy's eyes as she and Lucy had a conversation about the caves on Sullivan land, out near Bonsack river and the Bonsack mountain behind it. Dylan had bought the ranch outright. Therefore, he didn't know its layout or how much of the land was purchased in the deal. Lucy had mentioned that she,

Dennis, and Dylan had made maps of the land and exactly where those caves were.

Sophia didn't have a map on her. She didn't even know where they were kept. But she did know that when a five-year-old has an idea, his eyes tend to sparkle like moonlight off a bubbling brook. And that's just what happened to Muddy's little eyes.

She was ready to go in search of the caves, wishing only that she could get Owen to come along with her. Not hesitating another minute, Sophia made a beeline for Bonsack Mountain, which wasn't the tallest of mountains and might even be considered a large hill to people who lived near "real" mountains. But there were caves. Mostly small insignificant caves, temporary homes for some animal or another.

She shuddered to think of what would happen if a bear found a little human being and a tiny pig invading his home.

Her thoughts quickened her steps, and before she knew it, she was coming up on what looked like a big hole in the bottom of the mountain. She made a beeline for it, her heart thumping madly.

Please let him be there, she pleaded in her thoughts. *Please let him be there, oh, God, please.*

It was the closest one. It had to be the right one. He had to be in there. He just had to be.

She was nearly to it when the color baby blue caught sunlight at the entrance. It was Muddy's shirt. Sophia was overjoyed to see a little hand come out and rest against the mouth of the cave. At his feet, Sophia was sure she saw something pink.

She didn't want to get her hopes up, but what else could that be? She wasn't but twenty yards away when the little boy emerged from the cave and ran toward her.

"Sophiiieeeee," the boy cried out when he reached her, leaping into her arms.

"Oh, darling Muddy, where have you been? Everyone is worried sick about you."

"I came to show the caves to my new best friend, Barney." He looked down at his feet, where a tiny piglet was sitting. The animal was so calm and collected, looking around as if he hadn't a care in the world.

Sophia couldn't help squeezing Muddy tight. She tried hard to make it too hard, knowing the boy didn't like tight hugs.

"Are you ready to go home?" Sophia asked, taking Muddy's hand. "We'll have to run, and we'll have to stop and tell everyone on the other side of the river that you're safe. Come on now, let's see how quickly we can get home."

Muddy nodded, scooping up the piglet, who was surprisingly small. Sophia could definitely hold the piglet, though not for very long, as he was a solid little thing and probably weighed more than she expected.

"Are you hungry? I brought treats. I thought I might have to coax you or your new friend out of the jam you were in."

"I'm hungry," Muddy announced in response to her query. She pulled the flap up on her sack and dug through it with one hand.

She produced an apple with one hand and an orange with the other. Offering them to him, she said, "Here you go. Enjoy it. It looks like a storm is coming, so we have to hurry."

Muddy took the apple but said nothing to her as he bit into it. He closed his eyes and let out a satis-fied sound. His delightful smile made Sophia feel like a million. He kept his other hand locked in hers and didn't seem to mind when she dragged him over fallen trees and the like. She wanted to get back to the men as fast as possible.

To her astonishment, she halted in place as she watched something she'd never seen before.

The noise was deafening. Muddy cried out in fear. Sophia's heart quaked with the same as she witnessed the ground being ripped apart as if a seam was splitting open.

"Earth is quaking and shaking," Muddy called out, jumping up and down and clapping.

Sophia was not elated.

"We have to be extra careful now, Muddy," she called out over the noise of the earth splitting in half. "We should be able to get around it somehow. If not, we'll get back down to the river. That'll take us to the cabin and some clean, dry clothes." She didn't expect an answer from the little boy. She just wanted to get to the bridge again, and the men who needed to know Muddy had been found as fast as possible.

When it looked like the piglet was falling behind, Sophia scooped him into her arms.

"I'll keep you safe, Barney the Piglet, " she whispered affectionately.

Her arm was around the pig, and her hand was held by the child. All she needed now was a husband. She wanted a family. She wanted it with Owen.

Her heart leaped in her chest when she spotted him in the distance. He wasn't as far away as she'd thought he would be. Just seeing him again made her elated.

"Owen," she shrieked, knowing they were too far away to hear her. She stopped momentarily to throw her towel up in the air.

"Owen," Muddy cried out, mimicking her.

She giggled, glancing down at him. She bent slightly and wrapped an arm around his waist, lifting him up off his feet. She could go faster with him in her arm like the piglet.

"Owen," she called again, and Muddy said it with her this time.

Owen turned from the men he was with and saw her. Sophia could see plainly the look of astonishment on the faces of the men with Owen and on his face, as well.

He threw his arms up in the air, a huge smile covering his face. He began to run toward her.

He had to stop, sliding in the sand a bit when the earth rumbled violently beneath them.

Sophia stopped, too, looking down at her feet, terror sliding into her chest and holding her breath hostage.

"Sophia, go left. Go left."

She looked up to see Owen throwing both his

arms to her left. She turned and darted that way, unsure why he thought that would be safe.

Behind her, the earth ripped apart right where she'd been, creating a huge crack in the ground that ran between her and the bridge, as well as the men.

And Owen.

21

Sophia couldn't believe what had just happened. She ran as hard and as fast as she could toward the bridge, but the boy and the piglet weighed her down. The sand was soft beneath her feet and didn't promote fast running. Her eyes were on the bridge. That's where she wanted to be most of all. She wanted to cross the bridge and at least set them down on the other side.

But where was safe? Would the earth continue to quake and break apart?

It didn't matter anyway. She didn't reach the bridge. To her astonishment, the crack stretched out in front of her. She skidded to a halt, watching with wide, frightened eyes as the earth opened up beneath the river, creating a stream of water falling into the depths of the earth. The sound was tremendous as the earth became unstable under the bridge.

"No, no, no..." she moaned, watching the structure of the bridge crack from the bottom up. She could see the bridge splitting into parts as the earth shifted below it.

Muddy screamed in fear and grabbed Sophia around her neck, burying his face so he couldn't see the wreckage of the bridge, their only means to safety.

Sophia could barely breathe with the tightness of the boy's arms around her neck, but she couldn't bring herself to say anything to him to stop it. He was scared. She understood that.

At that point, the piglet had had enough. It wriggled violently in Sophia's hands, so she couldn't keep a grip on it.

"Barney, stop," she cried out, trying to keep hold of the animal. "Stop. Stop!"

The piglet wormed his way out of her hands and flopped to the soft sand on his side. He was promptly back up on his feet. He swiftly turned in the opposite direction and ran off into the woods.

"Barney," Sophia called, stretching out one hand as if she could reach him somehow.

"Sophia." It was Owen, calling to her from the

other side of the crack in the ground. Her eyes darted in his direction. He was pointing up at the sky.

Sophia turned her eyes to the darkened sky and was stunned to see those clouds were filled with lightning bolts, crackling and threatening. The rain would come pelting down at them any moment now. It was as if the weather had suddenly decided to revolt. She had never seen an earthquake or experienced one firsthand before. And for the earthquake to happen at the same time as a sudden storm, she wondered if that was in the almanac.

"You have to find shelter," Owen was screaming, cupping his mouth with his hands so his voice would carry further over the gap in the earth and the high winds. "Follow the pig. Follow the pig."

Sophia saw sense in that argument, as an animal goes purely on instinct. She turned and ran after Barney. He had gone into the woods, and she couldn't see him anymore. She darted a glance over her shoulder to see what Owen was doing. He had followed the crack in the earth as far as he could, watching her run toward the trees. She wished he was with her, right by her side, helping her, giving her strength.

"Sophie, Sophie, I don't wanna die."

Muddy's tears were making her shoulder wet. She squeezed him with the arm she had wrapped around him. "We're not gonna die, Muddy," she said, injecting as much confidence in her voice as she could. "I'm gonna get you back to that cave you were in, what do you say? That's a good place to be when the weather is bad. You were smart to go there. Very smart."

Muddy's tears halted, and Sophia said a silent prayer of thanks. He lifted his head and gave her a curious look. "It was smart, wasn't it?" he asked, needing just a bit more reassurance.

Sophia forced a smile, giving him an affectionate look. "Yes, Muddy. Very smart. Why, I don't know what we would do if you hadn't gone there. I might not have known it even existed, and then where would we find shelter?"

"You would have found it, Sophie," Muddy replied, squeezing her in a hug. She was glad his grip on her wasn't as tight anymore. "I know you would have. You are smart, too."

Sophia's heart melted for him. "Thank you, Muddy. That's very sweet of you."

She saw the cave in the distance and made for it. She thought it had to be fairly safe since Muddy had been in there with the piglet and hadn't been scared out by any large animals. Then again, after what just happened, chances were good she and Muddy weren't the only ones looking for shelter. The sudden storm had likely caught everyone by surprise.

Praying that no animals had chosen the cave for shelter, she made for the opening as quickly as she could. As soon as she was inside, she searched just with her eyes to see if it was still safe. She saw no danger, but with the sky dark and the sun covered, she couldn't see very far back into the cave.

There was no other choice for her and Muddy, though. When the first raindrop hit her on top of the head, she knew they needed to be under shelter and inside the cave. She'd have to have faith that it would be okay.

The drop that hit Sophia was huge. Once she was inside and turned around to watch the rainfall outside, she was amazed by the size of the water droplets and how loud they sounded when they began beating the ground. It was like God had turned a bucket of water over and just poured it on the earth.

She sat on the part of the earth that had jutted out from the wall of the cave and pulled Muddy onto her lap. They sat there for a few minutes, watching the water come down in droves.

"I'm sorry your birthday was ruined by this weather, Muddy. Why did you run off and scare everyone the way you did? Didn't you know we'd be worried about you?"

Muddy nodded, looking her directly in the eyes. She could see how much he trusted her. He was a sweet little boy. She was glad she had a job she loved so much.

"I wasn't gonna be long," he protested. "I was just gonna get Barney and make him come back. But he was so fast. And I couldn't get him. He ran fast."

Sophia nodded. "Well, next time something like that happens, you be sure to come and find an adult. It doesn't have to be me or momma or papa, but you should always tell an adult before you go running off. Can you remember that for me?"

Muddy nodded, looking ashamed. "Do you still like me?"

Sophia giggled, wrapping her arms around him in a warm hug. "Of course I do, you silly boy. I love you like you're my own little one." She pulled back from him and tapped him lightly on the nose, making him smile. "Just try to be safer next time, more mindful. You really had us all very scared, you know."

"Now *I* am scared," Muddy replied, shivering and pushing himself against her side. She glanced out at the pelting rain.

"I know. Me, too. And it's okay to be scared. You just have to be strong enough to get through to the end. We're safe in here. Owen and the men will come and get us as soon as they can."

"I'll come find you next time, Sophie," Muddy said, his little voice weak and tired. "I'm sorry I ran away."

"It's all right, Muddy," Sophia cooed, brushing his dark hair back from his head and kissing his forehead. She put both arms around him and rocked forward and back gently. "It's all right. We're gonna be fine. The men will come for us when the storm ends. We'll be all right. Don't you worry now."

22

Owen could not believe what had just happened. He watched Sophia run with the boy in her arms, her face terrified but determined. He didn't turn back to the men until he couldn't see Sophia anymore.

Byron was talking to the other men, gesturing wildly with his hands. Owen ran back to him and heard the tail end of what he was saying.

"You two can handle that. We're gonna have to figure something else out for Sophia and Muddy."

"Sophia will find shelter for them at the base of the mountain, Owen," Luke said, turning his head when Owen joined them, a stern look on his young face. "There are a couple of caves out that way she can take him to. We don't have a lot of wild animals on this here mountain, but there are some."

"Where are they going?" Owen asked, turning his head to watch the two ranch hands Byron had been talking to head toward the water.

"Strong swimmers," Byron replied, his blue eyes flashing, his face anxious. "They're gonna try to get across the water."

"I don't think that's a good idea," Owen said quickly. "Hey. Hey!"

The two ranch hands heard him over the rushing winds and water. They jogged back to him.

"The ground under the water is open. That means the water is rushing into it. I don't know how far down that water goes, but if you get in there and can't fight the current or the undertow, it will drag you right down, and you'll end up in the middle of the earth. Don't attempt to swim across that water."

"Good God." Byron put it, shaking his head. "I didn't see that. Hard enough to believe we had an earthquake right before a—"

The rest of what he said was muted by the crashing sound of thunder ripping through the sky. A bolt of lightning accompanied it, lighting up the darkness of the cloudy sky.

"We gotta find shelter, too," Owen barked.

"Come on. Let's see how far this crack goes into the woods. Maybe we can get across it somewhere."

He started to run toward the trees, aware that the men were on his heels, running through the beach sand as fast as they could. Byron sprinted past him, his long legs stretching, his feet bouncing off the sand as if it was rubber.

He reached the trees first, and Owen followed his tracks. The men went into the woods almost in single file as a result.

The crack in the earth only widened as they got into the forest. It was chaotic as it was, trees down everywhere, the winds blowing hard against the ones that remained standing.

"Look," Byron called out. "A cave."

"Just in time!" Owen reacted to the sight of the cave, speeding up his pace to get there before he was completely soaked through to the bone. Without a way to warm up or dry off, he ran the risk of getting sick.

The rain began beating down seconds before the men entered the cave. Owen was grateful he'd only had a few of the massive drops hit the top of his head, splattering on his hat, sounding like a rock had hit him.

He took the hat off as soon as he was in the cave,

slapping it on his thigh to get the water off the top. "That was close," he murmured, glancing around their temporary shelter, wishing it was the shelter Sophia had chosen.

Then again, she couldn't have. She was on the other side of the crack the earthquake had made.

Owen pictured it in his mind. Some areas had been close together—almost close enough to jump but not quite. Other areas were wide and terrifying. No chance of crossing. Ever.

He went to the opening of the cave, standing back enough to not get wet but to feel the drift of moisture in the air. For a long while, what was probably ten minutes but felt like an hour, he could barely see as the water poured out in buckets onto the earth, creating mud on the dry Texas ground that was sure to make everything dirty for a while to come.

He crossed his arms over his chest, thinking about what this meant for the Sullivan ranch. The bridge would have to be rebuilt, but the water pouring into the opening into the earth couldn't be stopped by man. Would it ever fill up? Would the water pouring into it drain the river? What could be done to stop it?

The earthquake had changed the very landscape of the Sullivan property.

He didn't know if there was any damage to the house itself either. He hadn't even thought to look across the water to see if anything was happening on the other side. All he'd seen was Sophia, running toward him with a piglet under one arm and a little boy sitting on her hip.

He tried to keep down the fear in his heart.

"What are we gonna do, Owen?"

Luke had come up beside him. His hands were placed on his hips, and his eyes stared out at the beating water. "Byron says we could be here for a while. No tellin' how long this storm is gonna last. And that quake opened up a massive crater right in the middle of the property. We can't even get across to the other side."

"We'll have to find a way."

Luke sighed resignedly. Owen glanced at him. He shrugged. "I don't know, Owen. Just seems like this is pretty hopeless."

"Hopeless?" Owen didn't understand Luke's way of thinking. He raised one eyebrow. "Luke, we're in a cave during a storm. It ain't like we're on a secluded island in the middle of an ocean. We'll be fine. Just gotta figure out how to get back across the river once the weather clears up. I've been caught in a blizzard before. Talk about thinkin' yer gonna die. Chin up, buddy." He punched the ranch hand lightly on the arm. "We just gotta be patient, that's all."

Luke seemed satisfied with that answer. He backed off and went to where the other men were attempting to create a pit to start a fire. They were all gathering rocks and putting them in a thick circle into which several men were throwing twigs, sticks, and leaves.

Luke watched them. It was a good idea to try to create some warmth, and several of the men had gotten wet. Drying off was important to prevent sickness.

Where are you, Sophia? he thought, turning away from them. He wanted to go closer to the edge, but the rain was still coming down too hard, and he would have been drenched if he got any closer.

He pictured her in a cave just a few feet away from him. He imagined she was sitting against the wall to his left, wondering where he was. When this was over, he planned to make sure she knew exactly how he felt about her. He would tell her he'd fallen in love with her. She was, from that moment on, the most important person on the planet to him.

Owen was determined to make sure she knew

that. He almost didn't care if she didn't have the same feelings for him. He wished he didn't care. But he was very much hoping—and believing—that she felt the same way. Their dinner together had been wonderful. Owen had never been so comfortable with a woman before. He felt like he could tell her his deepest darkest secrets—if he had any.

The rain continued to blast the ground outside while Owen fantasized about living a future with Sophia by his side. He found a huge flat rock near the entrance of the cave and sat down, leaning forward with his elbows on his knees, staring out at the rain.

Maybe they would have a dozen kids. Where would they live? Would he have to buy a grand house for her? He doubted she would demand such a thing. Besides, it was something he wanted to do. He wanted to give her everything she could ever need or desire.

He could still see her running toward him, her arms full of her charges, a smile on her pretty face.

How he wished she had been just a little further up so that she could have run toward him without fear instead of having to veer off to the left. The earthquake had separated them.

Sophia couldn't bear the weight of Muddy on her arm anymore. She didn't know how much time had passed, but it was long enough for her arm to go numb where he was holding onto it. He had fallen asleep, probably from sheer boredom and exhaustion. She wished she could do the same.

She moved away from him slowly, lowering him gently to the spot she'd been sitting on. She stood up and stretched, looking down at the sleeping child. He was smaller than an average five-year-old, she surmised. All the other five-year-olds who had attended his party had been bigger than him. Thank goodness they didn't bully him because of it, though

Sophia had a feeling the little boy might find that changed if he didn't grow big and strong like his father.

Sophia didn't know if she'd be around to see that happen since she was keen to start a family of her own. She couldn't imagine she would leave Bighorn, though, and hoped that if she ended up with Owen as her husband and father to her children, he wouldn't want to leave Bighorn either.

The rain outside seemed to lighten up a bit. Sophia could tell because it wasn't as loud. The lightning had ceased, and the rumbling of thunder had grown distant. The storm was passing.

Sophia pondered just how long she should wait before going out. She was still thinking about it when she was astonished to see sunlight. She blinked, her breath shallow. She walked slowly toward the entrance to the cave.

Poking her head out, she looked up and had to squint at the bright sun that had dipped low in the sky, preparing to retire for the night and let the moon take over. It was sending streaks of light through the wet trees, creating sparkles and rainbows all around her. For a moment, she thought how pretty it was.

Then she focused on the devastation the insane weather had caused to the land.

Sophia glanced back at her sleeping charge before stepping out of the mouth of the cave into the mud surrounding it. Trees of all sizes had been downed, huge limbs had broken off, and the ground had caved in around the gap the earthquake had made.

"I can't believe it didn't snow," Sophia murmured sarcastically. She couldn't get over the strange sudden violent weather.

She walked toward the crevice in the ground, reaching the edge and looking over. She couldn't see the bottom, but then again, she didn't expect to be able to. She'd never been so close to the edge of the earth before.

Shuddering, she stepped back and away from it. Her sea-blue eyes followed the crack from where she was back toward the mountain. It curved around when it got close to the mountain as if avoiding the massive mound of earth.

Her eyes landed on a speck of darkness in the distance, at the foot of the mountain. There was another opening there.

Sophia squinted. It was another cave. She thought she saw smoke coming out of it.

Frowning, she stepped to the side to attempt to get a clearer view. When she did so, tingles lit up around her body as she saw a man come to the entrance of the cave and look out.

It was Owen.

Her heart began to race. Her first instinct was to go back into the cave, grab Muddy and try to get to Owen. But second thoughts stopped her. If there was no way to get to Owen, it didn't make sense to wake up the sleeping child. That would run the risk of terrifying him all over again.

He was safe enough where he was, she decided, and if she hurried, she might be able to find a way to Owen before the child woke up. She ran back to the cave opening to check on him once more. He was still sleeping soundly, having turned over on his side with his hands beneath his head.

Relieved, Sophia spun around and returned to the edge of the cracked earth. She ran along the edge, looking ahead of her for a place that was not too wide for her to jump.

To her utter surprise, the crack swooped around and ended just before the other cave the men had gone into. Elated, Sophia continued to run, desperate to get to Owen and find a way to return to the ranch house. So far, no one had been hurt, at least not that she knew of. There was no telling, though, what had happened to the people at the house on the other side of the bridge.

Her heart leaped into her throat when Owen rested his eyes on her. The worried expression on his face turned to elation. His head darted to the side, and he yelled something to the men inside. A moment later, he was running toward her, and the men had all come out of the cave to watch the two reunite.

Sophia didn't care if they were being watched. She only cared about the fact that she and Muddy would be safer with the men than they would be alone. She was sure *someone* would think of a way across the river.

"Sophia. Sophia, thank God," Owen was calling out to her as they ran toward each other.

"Owen!"

They met in the middle, him wrapping his arms around her and her closing her eyes, pressing her body against his.

"Thank God you're all right," Owen said, holding her tightly. The next moment, he seemed to panic, pushing her away and looking into her eyes. "Where's Muddy? Is he okay? Is he safe?"

"He is. In that cave over there. Do you see it?"

She twisted her upper body to point back at the cave she'd just come from.

Owen squinted. She knew when he spotted the cave entrance because his face lit up. "Wonderful," he exclaimed. "We need to get him. Bring him to this one. The men have started a fire, and we're discussing how to get back to civilization and safety."

Sophia giggled. "You say back to civilization like we're on a deserted island in the middle of an ocean."

Owen gave her a strange look. "No, I'm just saying we don't have to go back to Sullivan ranch even if it's the closest to us. We can go around the mountain. Find another way."

"There are probably areas of the river that are narrow enough to get over across a fallen tree or something. Maybe you men can fashion a raft. Maybe—"

Owen laughed, stopping her words. He grabbed her shoulders and kissed her firmly on the forehead. "You have some good ideas, Sophia. Let's get Muddy and come back so you can tell them to the men, too, and not just me."

Sophia smiled at him warmly. "Okay."

Owen turned and called back to the men, "Goin' to get Muddy."

He gestured wildly in the air, jabbing one thumb in the direction Sophia had come from. Byron responded by lifting one hand and pointing one thumb to the sky.

"Come on," he said, taking hold of Sophia's arm and pulling her gently as he ran past where the gap from the earth separating began.

She willingly ran beside him, and when they got back to the cave, Muddy was in the same position he'd been in a few minutes ago when she'd left him behind.

She moved close to him and touched his cheek to wake him. He fluttered his eyelids.

"Let me get him," Owen said quietly, coming up behind her. He lowered himself, so he was eye-to-eye with the child. "Muddy," he whispered. "I'm gonna pick you up. Gonna take you somewhere a little safer. Don't be afraid, okay?"

In response, the very sleepy little boy reached out and put his arms around Owen's neck. Owen gently scooped the boy up in his arms. He nodded at Sophia, and they left the cave for the other one.

Sophia was glad Owen had told Muddy the place where they were going was a "little" safer. Like the rest of them, Sophia was sure Muddy wouldn't feel completely safe until he was in his own home, his own bed, with his loving family around him.

24

———————

It seemed to Owen like the moment the three of them entered the cave where the fire was lit and the men were sitting around it talking, the sky opened up, and more rain pelted the earth. A moment ago, they had seen the sun dipping behind the mountains, bringing in the dusk.

Now, though he couldn't see it as easily as before, Owen noticed the sky was once again covered in clouds. Had the storm reversed itself and decided to give them another go?

Muddy was asleep again almost immediately, this time in the arms of one of the bigger ranch hands. Patrick had a great beard and mustache that didn't hide the bright smile he had for others. Sophia told Owen quietly that she was content leaving Muddy in the care of the man, who had three boys of his own that he loved dearly.

Trying not to stare or be caught staring, Owen gazed at her as she held a conversation with Luke and Byron. She had a lovely profile. Her features fit together so well, he couldn't imagine a woman having a more perfect face.

She glanced at him, catching him staring at her. He blushed, feeling his face grow hot, but didn't look away, hoping she didn't notice it in the dimness of the firelight alone. He couldn't tell if she did or not. She scooted closer to him, where he was leaning against the wall with his legs spread out in front of him.

"They think my idea of building a raft is a good idea, too, did you hear?"

He nodded, smiling at her. "I thought they would." He pulled a handful of rocks from the ground by his side and began tossing the pebbles toward the fire.

"I guess we're going to spend the night in here, though, aren't we?" she went on. He looked at her again, amused by her excitable nature.

"Yeah, looks like it." He wished they were alone. He wished it was the first night of their honeymoon. Internally, he had to laugh. He hadn't even come close to asking the woman to be his sweetheart, and he was already thinking of their honeymoon. What if she was a terrible nag? What if she was a filthy person, never cleaning up after herself?

His thoughts further served to amuse him, as he had no doubt she was neither of those things. She was a responsible, smart, energetic woman who took care of three small children belonging to someone else. He couldn't imagine anything at all being wrong with her.

"Do you mind if I stay close to you?" Sophia asked.

Owen kept himself from snorting at the ridiculous notion that he wouldn't want her near him.

He nodded. "I'd like it if you did. Muddy is safe. You should be, too."

She grinned, scooting a little closer to him. It made his heart jump in his chest and begin to beat a little more rapidly. She gazed up at him, biting her bottom lip. "It probably won't get cold in here. I just hope it doesn't start to snow out there. It seems like we're getting hit with all kinds of things at once. Maybe a flood is next?"

"Hush," Owen scolded in a teasing voice, "don't say things like that. That's a lot of rain out there for the dry Texas ground to absorb. If it doesn't stop, a flood is the next step. So hush."

She giggled. "You are right. I am from Virginia, so I should have thought of that. I've been in a flood before."

"I'm sure it was terrifying."

"It was."

He couldn't take his eyes from her. She turned her head and looked into the fire. It danced off her slender face and made her eyes sparkle. Owen couldn't see getting any sleep that night. His heart was racing, his blood pumping, all he wanted to do was force the sun to come out, dry up the rain and let them get on with their lives.

"You know, we might not have to build a raft or anything like that," Sophia said in a voice that was obviously loud enough for the rest of the men to hear. They all looked at her.

"What are you thinking?" Byron asked.

Sophia shrugged. Owen had never been prouder of someone other than himself. "Well, it's not like the folks at the ranch didn't see where we'd gone. I'm sure they are going through their own trials or at least were, hopefully not now, and they will send help in the morning when it's light. Staying in here overnight is probably the best idea we could have had."

The men murmured to each other. Owen saw several of them nodding. They agreed with Sophia, and so did he. His unjustified sense of pride only grew at that point.

"You're right," he said, validating Sophia's thoughts. "I'm glad we're all in the one cave, though. I hate to think of how frightened you and Muddy would have been all night long by yourselves without a fire or anything."

Sophia sighed, giving him a grateful look. Her lips adorned a tiny smile, and Owen had to push away the urge to grab her and kiss her. It was getting harder and harder not to give in to that desire.

The rain quieted down a few minutes later. Sophia had gone quiet, and Owen had to look down to see if her eyes were still open because she was leaning against him. She was still awake, her eyes on the fire. He wondered what she was thinking about.

"Would you like to go see if the rain is lessening up a bit?" he whispered to her.

She turned her head to look up at him. "Yeah, let's do that," she whispered back.

They got up quietly so as not to disturb the men around them. Several had curled up on the ground, their hands under their heads or their hats providing a little cushioning from the hard ground. Two of the ranch hands were sleeping sitting up. Owen hated to think of the headache and neck pain they would have in the morning.

It was drizzling when he stuck his hand out to feel for rain. He stepped closer to the mouth of the cave and looked out at the sky. The clouds looked thin, enough for him to see through them with the moonlight alone.

"I would be relieved to see that," he said, "but it came back once before. It might come back again."

"I don't want to think about that," Sophia replied sternly. "We've got enough to do in the morning just getting back to the river around that crack in the earth. At least the quake didn't happen again. I wonder how much of Texas felt that?"

"There was no aftershock, at least we can say that. And it looks like... I've been picturing it in my mind as if I could see it from above based on what we can see down here." He lifted one hand and made a swoop in the air. "I think it looks like this. And that might mean that it's isolated to this area right here."

"Right where we happened to be," Sophia mentioned sarcastically.

He gave her an agreeable look. "Exactly," he said. "The good thing about that is that it might not have touched the ranch house, and everyone there is safe. The only reason I don't think that's the case is that they haven't sent anyone to look for us yet. Have you heard anyone calling out for us? Seen any lights from lanterns or torches?"

Sophia shook her head, her eyes directly on him as she listened.

"No, I haven't either. And to me, that means they can't. They would have. I'm sure of it."

"I think you're right," Sophia agreed. "We won't know until the morning, though. I would say that we should go in and get some rest, but I'm wide awake. I feel like walking around and seeing what I can do to get home now, but..." She lifted one hand and gestured at the scene in front of them. "It's a little bit dark. I can't see. No sense in causing myself more problems."

Owen couldn't help chuckling. "You're right. I feel the same if I'm honest with you. We'll have to practice what we preach and be patient, I guess."

The look she gave him made him feel tingly inside. "Yes," she responded. "We'll have to wait until daylight."

25

Owen was the first one to wake up the next morning. He was up as soon as the light hit the inside of the cave and his eyes. There were stirrings among the other men. Sophia hadn't fallen asleep until after him. He was sure he'd seen her awake, staring into the fire, as his last memory from the night before.

She'd fallen asleep with her head against his arm. The only way he could get up was to move her gently, so she was leaning against the wall. She grunted and moved until she was comfortable. It still didn't look comfortable to him, but she stayed asleep, amazingly enough.

He got to his feet and went to the mouth of the cave to look out at the sky and the sun. Both were bright, warm, and dry. There were no clouds as far as he could see.

The suddenness of the storm's onset was what had Owen upset. He knew there was nothing he could do about it, but he couldn't help wishing there was a way to be more precise about the weather. A way to predict when things like this would happen so people wouldn't be caught off guard.

He stepped out into the already drying mud, making a mental note that he would dedicate his future—at least some of it—to finding ways to predict weather patterns more accurately than the almanac. It was good to base predictions on weather patterns of the past, but it just wasn't enough. More had to be done. Lives could be saved.

The earthquake weighed heavily on Owen's mind. There was no prediction of that. He wasn't aware, after studying the history of the area before coming to work in Bighorn, of any earthquakes happening in this particular part of Texas. Earthquakes were known to happen in the state—but not around Bighorn.

He'd gone back ten years in almanacs for the area and had not seen one earthquake mentioned in all of them.

"What's it look like to you?" He heard Byron

behind him. He glanced back at his friend, who looked sleepy and stressed, his blond hair in a jumble on his head, sticking up in some places, laying flat in others.

"Looks like a big heaping mess," he replied. He jabbed one thumb over his shoulder at the devastation behind him, "and that looks pretty bad, too."

Byron snorted, lowering his eyelids at Owen. "Hyuk, hyuk," the man stated darkly.

Owen chuckled, looking back at the wreckage around him. "I think we're gonna be making new trails to get back to the river. We might have to build that raft after all. We've got the supplies right here." He spread his arms out wide to take in everything in front of him. "Even got vines to use for rope."

"I don't think we need to do all that," Byron said. We ought to just find our way back to the river and stay there until someone sends a rescue boat. It's not that hard to get across the river. It can't be more than fifty yards wide at the widest spot. Ten yards at others. If it wasn't so deep, we could walk across."

Owen nodded. He hadn't known that information about the river and was glad Byron assumed he did.

His stomach growled loudly, reminding him it had been a long time since he'd eaten. He imagined they would hear more about that subject when Muddy was awakened. He was a little surprised the boy wasn't awake already.

Looking back into the cave, he saw that Patrick was awake. He had sat up but was still holding the child on his lap, and Muddy was using the big man as a pillow. Patrick didn't seem to mind. He gave Owen a smile when their eyes met.

"Let's go see what it looks like," Owen said, waving to Byron to follow him.

The two men walked first to the huge gap in the ground. Some parts of the edges had fallen in, creating the haphazard look of a crater, as if something had hit the ground instead of the earth splitting itself in two. The most astonishing thing was that it had filled with water.

Owen knelt by the edge on one knee, bracing himself before looking over into the still water.

"You think something came from the sky and hit the ground right here?" he asked. "Maybe it wasn't an earthquake, after all." He couldn't see anything in the middle of the crater.

"I felt the ground rumbling under me," Byron responded. "Didn't you?"

Owen nodded. He had felt that. But the impact of the object hitting the earth could have caused that, couldn't it? He looked up. Was it possible for something to come from the sky and make a hole and a crack this big in the earth?

He didn't see why not. Maybe it was a star. Maybe this was what happened when one of those twinkling bits in the dark velvet sky of the night decided it was done. He had no clue. His ideas about the earth and the sky were all based on his assumptions of how things were. He'd learned as much as he could while in school. But it seemed no one really had the answers he wanted to questions that were important to him.

"I reckon something might have fallen out of the sky," Byron spoke up, scratching the side of his beard. He didn't sound very confident in his words. Owen got the feeling he agreed because Owen seemed determined to find out what really happened.

Owen stood up straight again, proceeding to follow the new line of the river until they were back out on the shore, in sight of the destroyed bridge once again.

He visualized what had happened the day before when he'd seen her running to him with the boy and the piglet. It came to him so clearly in his mind.

"Look, Owen."

He turned his head to see Byron heading toward the bridge. "It doesn't look like the bridge has been completely destroyed. We might be able to get over it after all."

Owen was a little irritated that they hadn't investigated it the night before, but he reminded himself that the second wave of the storm had kept them inside the cave. It was still raining when they'd gone to sleep. Not as heavy as at first, but it was still raining. The rain would have put out any torches they tried to light to see in the dark.

Satisfied that this was the earliest opportunity they'd had to check the bridge, Owen followed his friend onto the rickety structure. They moved carefully, stepping one foot in front of the other, Byron testing the boards in front of him to make sure they could handle his weight before taking the next step forward.

They were nearly at the top of the arch when Owen saw the problem. There was a gap, much like the one in the earth that had caused this devastation to begin with. Except this one hadn't filled with water and still posed a big problem for them if they wanted to go across.

"Well, it will be easier to figure out how to get from here to there than it was to get from there to there." Byron moved his hand, gesturing from one side of the river to the other.

"Let's go back and tell them the good news," Owen said, suddenly feeling a rush of urgency to get back across the river to the ranch house. If something had fallen from the sky and caused the crack in the earth, there would be no mention of an earthquake among the people back at the house.

Maybe someday he would swim own into that new part of the river and see if anything was down there. A small smile lifted the corners of his lips when he thought about what an adventure that would be.

He wondered if Sophia would go with him.

26

———

Sophia was awake soon after Owen left the cave. She only knew that because she heard him outside talking to Byron. She glanced over to see Muddy was still on Patrick's lap, and the big man was having a quiet conversation with another ranch hand.

She slid her eyes to the mouth of the cave and spotted a sleeping Barney just inside it, pressed up against a rock. She tilted her head and gave the animal an affectionate glance. He'd found them after all. She was glad he was safe.

She pushed to her feet and went toward the fire, where logs were burning in bright red embers, but there were no real flames. For a moment, she pondered if she wanted to build the fire at all. They would be leaving soon, surely. The sun was up, and the sky was clear.

The devastating weather of the day before was done. Whatever had happened, she was alive and no one had been hurt.

There was a small pile of sticks and twigs near the firepit. Sophia hesitated just another moment before grabbing the sticks and pushing them into the burning embers. It didn't take long for the flames to lick quietly up toward the ceiling of the cave.

She stood there for a moment, watching the fire dance around. When Owen came back, he would have a report and probably a solution for how they could get home. It wasn't long before he was back, strolling through the cave entrance, his eyes intent on her.

"Come look at this," he said in a low voice.

Sophia's curiosity peaked. She hurried after him, dropping the stick she'd been poking the fire with. He took her to the edge of the huge hole in the ground the earthquake had caused. She saw that it had widened in that spot, with much of the earth falling in. She was astonished to see the hole had filled up with water.

"Does this mean the crater has a bottom?" she asked.

Owen looked at her soberly. "It must. It couldn't have filled up with water otherwise. And it's filled with water all the way to the part where we crossed over the bridge. And the bridge isn't completely broken. It is split in half, and we do have to figure out how to get over that gap, but it's possible. It's possible."

Sophia wondered if he was trying to convince her or himself when he repeated the sentence.

"I want to see it."

When Owen took her hand to lead her to the bridge, Sophia's entire arm erupted in tingles. Her heart jumped and began to race. She squeezed his hand and was delighted when he glanced over his shoulder at her with a smile, squeezing back.

She was happy to see the bridge was not as destroyed as she thought it was. She'd pictured in her mind the entire thing dropping into the water. It had split in the middle, though, leaving jagged edges on both sides that looked sharp and just as dangerous as the gap between them.

She studied the scene, looking for ways to get over the gap. They could get a fallen tree and set it over the gap, then climb over it very carefully. She turned her head to tell Owen that when he said, "I think our best bet is still to wait until someone comes on the other side and helps us. They can bring a ladder to set over the gap like this." He gestured with his hand, and Sophia visualized it, nodding.

"You're right. That's a good idea. They will have supplies. But what do we do? Just sit here and wait for someone to show up?"

Owen chuckled. "I can't imagine we'd have to wait long. They've got to be pretty frantic over there. You know how Dylan is about his sons. I wouldn't be surprised if a doctor had to give him a sedative to help him stay calm last night. He doesn't know if his son is even still alive."

"You're right again." Sophia nodded. She could see Dylan in her mind, losing his mind over his missing son. It only made her want to return Muddy to his parents quickly even more.

"I'm going back to get Muddy," she said in a determined voice. "We all need to come out here and wait. Maybe that fellow who wanted to swim yesterday will want to again today."

Owen's eyes lit up. "That's right." We could send at least one of them boys over there. The water has calmed down since yesterday. Let's go get them."

Sophia was proud that he appreciated her suggestion. She jogged back to the cave with him, her eyes running over the newly formed arm of the river. It was shaped like an apostrophe, with a big round space near the caves and a swooping arm jutting directly into the original body of water.

Muddy was just waking up when she got back. He was sitting on Patrick's lap with a dazed look on his face. His eyes were open, but Sophia was willing to bet he was still in a dream state.

She went to Patrick and knelt in front of the sleepy boy.

"Good morning, little master," she said in a sing-song voice. She held out her arms to him. When his eyes focused on her, he brightened up some and leaned forward, falling off Patrick's lap into her arms. She caught him neatly with a smile. "We're gonna go home now," she said quietly. "You want to?"

He nodded. "I want Momma," he murmured, lowering his head to Sophia's shoulder. She lifted him up as she stood up and propped him on her hip again.

"I know you do, honey. And that's where we're going."

"Momma... Papa..." Muddy sighed heavily as if he was never to see his parents again. Sophia's heart went out to the little boy. He'd been through so much on his fifth birthday.

She carried him out into the bright sunlight. Once the sun hit him, Muddy seemed to wake up and brighten up. He lifted his head from her shoulder and squinted, looking around as if he didn't know where he was or what was going on. Then he pushed away from her, and she knew he wanted to get down.

"We're going to the bridge," she directed him as she set him on his feet. "It's over there. That's where we need to go now, okay? Don't go anywhere else but there. That's going to take us home."

Muddy ran off from her.

"Be careful," she cried out, picturing him stumbling forward and scraping up his hands and knees.

He didn't fall, however, and before she knew it, she was at the bridge with him.

The little boy had stopped before taking a step onto the broken bridge. He was staring at it skeptically as if he thought it might break into bits if he put a foot forward.

Sophia took his hand and stepped forward. He

watched her feet and his own as he walked carefully forward onto the structure.

"It's safe," she said softly. "It's broken in the middle, but it's bearing up to the weight just fine."

Muddy looked bewildered but walked slowly beside her. His hand gripped hers until they were at the edge. Muddy didn't get too close. He lifted up on his little toes and looked over.

"That's scary," he said, scooting closer to Sophia.

She put one arm around him and held him against her leg. "It is," she admitted, "but as long as you're careful, you won't fall over and into the water. It's deep. You don't want to fall in."

Muddy looked up at her. "I can't swim," he said, his eyes big with wonder.

Sophia nodded. "I know. And we'll make sure by the time you're six you can, okay?"

He grinned. "Okay."

"Sophia!"

She turned to see Owen was calling her. She wasn't willing to leave Muddy on the bridge alone, even if he knew he could get hurt if he fell over. He was five. He couldn't yet be trusted not to follow his instincts.

The two walked back down to Owen, who was

standing with one of the young men who would have swum the river the night before.

"Jacob is gonna swim across and go get help," Owen said, clapping one hand on the young man's shoulder. "So we don't have anything to worry about anymore." He bent down, so he was face to face with Muddy. "You're gonna be back with Momma and Papa real soon. I promise."

Muddy was the first one to go over on the boat that was brought out to the lake. Sophia watched as the several men from the party the night before came stomping through the woods carrying the small johnboat on their shoulders. Mattie and Dylan were behind the men with the boat, and behind them were Lucy, who was holding Collin on one hip and Felix on the other, and the family that owned Barney.

Sophia wondered if the family had stayed over or come early in the morning. She also couldn't help wondering if they were really that concerned about the piglet, which led to her hiding giggles behind her hand.

Sophia stood with Owen in silence as the ranch

hands rowed the boat back to the other side, with Muddy standing at the very front like George Washington crossing the Delaware. The boat hadn't reached the shore completely before Mattie and Dylan splashed out into the water, their arms outstretched, their cries of joy ringing out through the air. They grabbed the little boy from the boat and splashed their way back to shore, laughing and hugging and crying.

Sophia held back her tears watching them. She sniffed a little, and Owen chuckled. She looked at him. He raised his eyebrows.

"I didn't say anything," he said, holding up his hands. "It's a touching scene. I'll give you that."

"I can't believe we just went through that," Sophia remarked softly.

She felt tingles when he put one arm around her shoulders and left it there as if claiming her as his own. She didn't mind that at all.

They stood there watching as everyone went across. Eventually, it was just her, Owen, and Byron.

"Byron," Owen said his friend's name in a voice that spoke volumes. He'd had an idea, and Sophia was anxious to hear what it was.

"Yes, sir?" Byron replied humorously.

"I'm gonna row Sophia and me around for a bit on the river. You don't mind, do you?"

Byron pulled his eyebrows together and gave Owen a confused look.

"Uh, no? Why would I mind?"

Owen shrugged. "Well, you'll have to walk all the way back through the woods all by yourself. Think you can do that?"

Byron laughed, recognizing his friend was joking. "I think I can. Thanks. You're not gonna make me swim across, though, right? I mean, the three of us can fit in the boat until we get to the other side."

Sophia was giggling at the silly conversation between the men. She liked the way their friendship was on full display whenever they were around each other.

"I reckon we can wait until you're on the other side before we start our good time together. If we have to."

Owen sighed heavily, but a smile came to his face immediately after. Both men headed toward the boat, and Sophia hurried to keep up with them.

Once they were on the other side, Byron stepped out into the wet sand. He turned back to push them off and waved with a smile.

"Have fun. Don't get caught in any storms. You ain't got the supplies for that."

Sophia laughed as the boat drifted away from the shore, and Owen took up the oars to direct it down the riverbed away from the broken bridge.

"He's a humorous man," she said appreciatively. "You two are good friends, aren't you?"

"Yeah, he's the first friend I made when I came here to Bighorn," Owen replied. "We get along really well. I trust him. That's what's most important in a friendship, don't you think?"

He was giving her such an intense look it made her insides feel warm, and her heartbeat sped up. "I do think so," she agreed with a nod. She leaned over and ran her hand over the top of the water. There was a lot of debris from the night's storm floating on the surface, flowing with the slow current. Her fingers pushed aside small twigs, lots of leaves, flowers, petals, and other natural fragments.

"You were so brave what you did yesterday, Sophia," Owen said, his admiration plain on his face and in his voice. "I was really impressed."

Sophia had never been complimented that way before. She blushed furiously, feeling her face become hot.

"Oh, and you look amazing when you're blushing," he continued quickly. "I'm going to have to compliment you more, so you do that more often. You are a beautiful woman, you know. Gorgeous, in my estimation. I want to spend more time with you. As much time as I can. I hope I'm not being too forward by telling you this. I... I mean every word of it."

Sophia didn't know how to respond. Her mind was jumbled with all the words she wanted to say. She couldn't just open her mouth and speak because she was afraid it would come out sounding dumb, and she would feel like a fool.

"I... I feel the same way," she said, choosing the most basic words to say in response. "I really do. I want to spend time with you, too."

How could she tell him she'd been thinking about them getting married and having children together? How could she say she had dreamed when she was young of meeting a man just like him, a kind, compassionate, smart man who wanted good for others as well as himself?

Could she just blurt those words out?

She had a feeling if she did, it wouldn't scare him away. The intense way he stared at her made her heart shake in her chest. It was hard to breathe. She lifted one hand and waved it at her face.

"Suddenly, I feel very hot," she said weakly.

Owen stopped rowing and leaned toward her. "Are you all right? You didn't catch something being in that weather last night, did you?"

Sophia pulled herself together, taking in a deep breath and holding it for a moment. She closed her eyes momentarily and then opened them, determined to see this moment through to the fullest.

"The only thing I've caught is love," she said, immediately regretting it. It sounded stupid. It was idiotic. He would think she was a fool.

Her breath was shaky now. She would start trembling at any moment. Maybe she would just lose her balance and fall into the water. That would complete her foolish appearance, wouldn't it?

"Love for me?" he asked, not laughing or teasing.

She swallowed. "Yes," she breathed.

Even though Owen didn't immediately say anything, Sophia knew it wasn't because he didn't want to hear what she said. It wasn't because he didn't feel the same way. She had a feeling it was because he, like her, wasn't sure exactly what to say.

He proved her to be right when he held out his hand to her, letting one of the oars prop itself on the side of the boat where it was connected through a loop.

She took it, enjoying the thrill his touch gave her and hoping that feeling lasted for years and years.

"I caught the same thing," he said softly, gazing directly into her eyes. "But my love is for you, not me."

He gave her a quick grin, which made her heart sing. Gone was the uncomfortable feeling of looking foolish. He had taken her seriously and responded in the exact way she wanted him to.

"You love me?" she whispered, leaning toward him, too.

His grin returned. "Yes," he answered. "I do love you."

Sophia swallowed hard, fighting the tears of happiness that threatened to fall. She didn't want him to think she was a sensitive little girl. She'd been through a lot in her life. To finally feel the love that she'd longed for, like every other little girl in the world, was an amazing experience.

"Sophia, the next time I bring you out on this boat, it will be with a picnic basket on a clear, sunny day when the almanac doesn't predict a sudden storm."

Sophia giggled. "I'd like that."

"In fact, it will be around a time when there is

absolutely no chance of a storm for at least a month in either direction forward or back."

Sophia's giggles turned to laughter.

"We might be waiting a while for that. What if it's in the middle of December?"

He laughed with her. "Then we'll just have to wear thick coats for our picnic and eat with our mittens on."

28

It was a hot and sweaty day in the middle of August. Owen was anxious to get home and take a bath. The night was promising to be a special one since Mattie and Dylan were planning to announce some big plans they had for expanding the ranch. They'd prepared a big celebration, which they were holding inside.

Dylan had mentioned at least twice to Owen that it would be a while before he and Mattie had another party outside. Their land hadn't been touched by the earthquake. In fact, the spot on the other side of the river where it happened was the only sign that the earth had rumbled at all.

Owen thought about that as he walked from the barn he'd been working at with Byron to the bunkhouse. They'd cut off work at four, so they would have time to prepare for the party. As usual, Dylan had invited all of the ranch hands, plus the indoor staff, to attend as guests.

It had been a busy summer. Most of it had been taken up by rebuilding the bridge across the river and building a second one in case the first one broke again. The second one was down at the end of the Sullivan property. If something happened to either bridge, it simply meant a longer walk to get home.

Dylan had also decided to put a supply barn on the other side of the river. He said it paid to be cautious, and they all agreed with him.

Owen hadn't consulted Dylan about it, but he was sure his boss wouldn't mind if he did some research into what really happened that night of the storm. He'd long since thought it was too much of a coincidence that the earth had shook and split that way, and the storm had been so bad. There was so much about what was above them in the sky that they just didn't understand.

Owen wanted to understand. He wanted to look up into the heavens and look closely at the clouds and stars and see what they were made of. He wanted answers. He wanted to know what was on the surface of the moon. What was it like up there?

Was there room to move around? Air to breathe? There had to be more to the stars in the sky than just the twinkling lights.

And the crater that had filled with water, what had caused it? For all the reports Owen had read since it happened, he was yet to find one that created a crater like the one on the Sullivan land. None of the other quakes had affected one isolated spot. They didn't end up looking like an apostrophe.

They were long, and the devastating effects were felt for miles and miles around. The people at the ranch house hadn't even known what had happened. They'd told Owen and Sophia they felt rumblings under their feet but didn't even think of an earthquake. They thought it was the effects of the terrible storm.

By the time Owen got back to the bunkhouse, he was ready to take a swim. He would rather go out to the apostrophe and try to figure out if something hit the ground there than take a bath in the bunkhouse, waiting his turn.

He carried a pair of short pants along with him to the river. It was a fairly long walk, and he was ready for it, but he got as far as the back lawn when he stopped. Sophia was sitting at one of the lawn tables with Lucy and the children. He had to take a moment to think about what a beautiful woman she was and how proud he was that she was to be his wife eventually.

He approached from behind her quietly. Lucy looked up and saw him, but she dropped her eyes immediately as if she hadn't seen him there. He came up silently behind Sophia and wrapped his hands around her eyes.

"Guess who?" he asked, leaning close and kissing her temple.

"I think if that isn't Owen, somebody might be getting slapped in a moment," she replied in a laughing voice.

He chuckled, moving around so she could see it was indeed him.

"No slapping necessary," Owen said quickly, trying to look scared. She just laughed, and he knew he looked more ridiculous than scared.

"You are going to the new watering hole, aren't you?" she asked, running her eyes up and down his body.

He looked down at himself. "Yes. I think I'm going for a swim. You have time to come along?"

Sophia turned to look at Lucy, who grinned and nodded. "Collin will be down for a nap soon, and

Felix will be right behind him. Muddy and I can find some fun things to do, can't we, Muddy?"

The little boy grinned big from where he was sitting on a blanket spread out on the ground near them. "We can," he responded brightly.

"Wonderful." Sophia pushed herself to her feet, her eyes on Owen. "Wait here. I'll be right back."

She ran off toward the house. Owen sat in the chair she'd abandoned.

"You know, you two have to be really careful out there swimming in that crater," Lucy said in a pondering voice. "You could get hurt. You don't know what's in that water."

Owen frowned. "It's river water, Lucy. It's not poisonous."

"But you said you think something fell from the sky and made that hole, and the only reason it filled up with water is that the earth cracked right into the river where the water already was."

Owen was impressed with how well Lucy had apparently been listening. She repeated back to him nearly verbatim what he'd originally said.

"Yes, that's true. But if there was something in the water from whatever it was, if that's even what happened, that would mean all the water in the river and the ocean would also be poisonous. I don't think that's the case since the fish are still swimming."

Lucy blinked rapidly. He had a feeling she'd been holding onto that fear for the last couple of months and had only now just had it explained to her. She looked satisfied and a little relieved. He was glad to see it.

Sophia was out of the house just a few minutes later. Owen was pleased with her eagerness to explore the newly formed arm of the river. Maybe they would find gold if they swam down far enough to find a vein.

Owen didn't say that out loud. It was a ridiculous —if not amusing—thought.

He held out his hand to her.

"You ready?" he asked.

"I'm ready," she responded, taking his hand. He pictured her doing that the day of their marriage. They would walk down the aisle together after the preacher said they were now man and wife.

Owen was looking forward to that day. More than anything.

29

The water was cool and refreshing. Sophia was happy to be experiencing it with Owen. She hadn't gone swimming much in her lifetime. There hadn't been time for such frivolities. Now that she was on the verge of getting married and having her own home and children, she was anxious to experience all the things she hadn't been able to when she was younger.

The crater filled with water wasn't the most fun ever. She liked to be on the regular beach and walk into the water or sit on the very edge and let it come up and splash around her. Owen liked to jump into the deep chasm in the earth and swim from side to side as fast as possible.

Sophia thought it was more fun to watch him than to participate in all that exercise.

She sat on the shore, her feet dangling in the water, watching him race back and forth, calling out for her to count the seconds it took for him to get from one side to the other. She was having a lot of fun telling him exaggerated numbers, asking him once if he was all right. He was gone so long she thought he'd drowned.

It was impossible for that to have been true because he was swimming across the surface, not underneath it. She could see him the entire time. He only laughed and told her she was not a very good counter.

When he tired of the swim, he came to where she was and pulled himself out of the water. She gave him a towel from the stack she'd brought from the house, and he dried his face with it.

"You like nature a lot, don't you?" she asked, studying his handsome face.

"I love it," he replied immediately, his eyes on her. "It's fascinating, don't you think? I know God created all this, but there's so much to learn about it all. So much we don't know that would just make things more interesting, you know? How many of these plants out here can we eat? Which ones are poisonous? Why are they poisonous and not the others? What makes that particular plant poisonous?" He shook his head. Sophia felt like she could see the gears in his brain moving. "It's not just the earth that I find so... so interesting. It's everything. The sun, the moon, the stars, the earth... it's all just amazing to me."

"You should be a scholar at a university."

Owen shook his head. "That's what the folks said, too. The problem with that is that I'd have to focus my attention on one thing. The one subject that I would teach as a professor. But I'm not one to stand in front of a classroom and teach and lecture. I want to be out in it, finding out these things on my own. I don't want to read it from a book." He smiled at her. "I want to be the one to *write* the book."

Sophia felt her heart nearly bursting with attraction for the well-spoken man. "I want to read it after you write it," she said. "I'm fascinated by those things, too, but I think I would rather be out in the field with you, learning from you, than in a classroom."

Owen nodded. "When I am old and gray and talking to our grandchildren, then I will be the professor and the lecturer. Until then, I want to be the doer, the adventurer, the one who experiences and learns it all firsthand so I can teach others from what I've learned myself."

Sophia was so impressed with him. She felt like she could sit by his side and listen to him all day, even though, at the time, the only fact he could give was that he was guessing at most of his theories. She agreed what he said made sense. It didn't seem plausible that the earthquake had only been a mile or so long and that it had curved in the earth, creating a swoop instead of a straight line. It was also a mystery that the largest part of the crevice was a large round hole—as if something had slammed into the earth and created it.

Sophia suddenly realized Owen had said he would tell "our" grandchildren the stories. Her heart nearly jumped out of her chest. As confident as she was that they would be married and live as a happy couple, eventually a family, for the rest of their lives, she still loved to hear him reference it.

"When we get married," Owen said, as if reading her thoughts, "we should have it here. On this land."

"The Sullivan ranch?" Sophia asked, glancing across the riverbed at the trees that blocked her view of the actual ranch house. "I'm sure they would let us."

"Oh, I know Dylan would," Owen replied. "But I

mean here. Right here. I'll get the men to put up a quick gazebo, and we'll have the ceremony right here."

"Hmmm." Sophia tilted her head to the side, examining his face closely. She narrowed her eyes at him. "You're being a little crazy about this place, aren't you? You aren't going to ask Dylan if we can build a house here, are you? I think it's a little scary here. I wouldn't want to live here."

Owen grinned. "No, no, I wasn't thinking of that. I just love the way it looks here. The sand is soft beneath our feet, the sky is clear above, not blocked by tree limbs and leaves, and there's plenty of space. But if you don't want to, that's okay. Somewhere else is fine. The only thing I want is to make you my wife. We can do that anywhere. In a basement cellar or in the cemetery or—"

"Owen." Sophia laughed, slapping his arm playfully. "We can do it here. That's all right with me. Just don't build us a house here. I don't want to be that close to water."

"No," Owen said again. "I wasn't even thinking about that." He stopped abruptly, lifting his eyes up. "Although now that you've mentioned it..."

He burst out laughing heartily when she cried out and swatted at him a little harder.

"I'm joking with you, Soph. I'm joking."

She laughed with him, happiness filling her chest and making her feel like crying. She had never felt so much love for another human being in all her life.

He seemed to sense that she was overwhelmed with her emotions because he stopped laughing and gave her a look of deep affection. "You're such a beautiful woman, Sophie. Inside and out. I'm so proud to have you in love with me. You're really going to marry me, aren't you?"

Sophia smiled wide. "Yes, Owen. I'm really going to marry you."

"I'm so excited." He said the words so plainly as if the opposite were true.

But Sophia knew better. She could see his love for her written on his face, deep in his eyes, hear it in his voice.

"Only another few weeks, and we will be man and wife," she murmured.

He didn't say anything back. Instead, he moved close to her, getting on his knees and taking her face in his hands. He lowered his head and pressed his lips against hers, sending a shock of emotions through her body. She wrapped her arms around his neck and pulled up to meet him, returning the kiss with all the passion she had in her.

"I love you," he whispered against her lips when they pulled apart.

"I love you, too, Owen," she whispered back before another kiss swept the words away.

Click here for more Blythe Carver books!

Sign up for the newsletter to be notified of new releases.

Click on link for
Newsletter
or put this in your browser window:

landing.mailerlite.com/webforms/landing/p6l2s1

www.ingramcontent.com/pod-product-compliance
Lightning Source LLC
Chambersburg PA
CBHW051154130726

47988CB00005B/2118